A PATRIOT'S ACT

KENNETH EADE

D1714286

Times Square Publishing

© Copyright 2015 Kenneth Eade

Third Edition

ISBN: 1530323711

ISBN 13: 9781530323715

OTHER BOOKS BY KENNETH EADE

Brent Marks Legal Thriller Series

A Patriot's Act

Predatory Kill

HOA Wire

Unreasonable Force

Killer.com

Absolute Intolerance

Decree of Finality

Espionage

An Involuntary Spy

To Russia for Love

Stand Alone

Terror on Wall Street

Non-fiction

Bless the Bees: The Pending Extinction of
our Pollinators and What You Can Do to Stop It

A, Bee, See: Who are our Pollinators and
Why are They in Trouble?

Save the Monarch Butterfly

In memory of J. Howard Standing,

My first associate in law

Patriotism is a kind of religion; it is the egg from which wars are hatched.

-Guy de Maupassant

Voice or no voice, the people can always be brought to the bidding of the leaders. That is easy. All you have to do is tell them they are being attacked, and denounce the peacemakers for lack of patriotism and exposing the country to danger. It works the same in any country.

– Hermann Goering

Democracy is not freedom. Democracy is two wolves and a lamb voting on what to have for lunch. Freedom comes from the recognition of certain rights, which may not be taken, even by a 99% vote.

- Marvin Simkin

PART I

THIS ISN'T WHAT THE GOVERNMEANT

CHAPTER ONE

Ahmed felt the butt of the rifle strike his spine between his shoulder blades as his knees buckled, and he hit the floor. The sensation of falling was even stranger because he couldn't see anything. It was as if he were in slow motion, spiraling out of control.

His hands were shackled behind his back, so there was no way to break his fall. He landed on his side, slamming his shoulder into the cold concrete floor. He could feel the fibers of the black hood against his lips, and smell the sweat of the last person who had been forced to wear it. He stood up and started to walk again.

"Move faster Haji!" commanded an authoritative voice in a Southern American drawl. Ahmed felt the rifle butt hit hard against his spine again and he shuffled faster, within the confines of his ankle chains, which allowed only a minimum of movement. Thoughts of his wife Catherine, her silky brown hair, soft brown eyes and captivating smile, and their two small children, Karen and Cameron, back in their home in Santa Barbara, flooded his brain. These thoughts were the only thing lately that kept him sane.

"Up against the wall! – Stop there! Up against the wall I said – now!"

Ahmed stopped and did as he was commanded.

"Listen up!" barked a mechanical voice in the darkness, "My name is Sergeant Brown. You have been placed in my custody. You're here because you have refused to cooperate in interrogations. The decision has been made to execute you by firing squad."

"Wait!" said Ahmed, "I'm an American citizen."

"Sure you are, A-hab."

"My name is Ahmed."

"Your name is A-hab. A-hab the A-rab and the only thing I need to hear from you today is whether you want your mask on or off."

"Off."

Ahmed felt the black bag ripped from his head and, for the first time, faced his aggressors. The man who had ripped off his bag was a young man in military camouflage fatigues, holding an M16 to his chest. In front of him was an eight-man firing squad, also in camouflage fatigues, with rifles at their sides in ready position. Standing at their side was obviously Sergeant Brown, a hefty black man with huge hands, the only one not holding a weapon. For a 25-year-old man like Brown, who was always inept in every way outside the service, power was orgasmic. He basked in it like the sun, as if he was on a white sand beach in Maui.

Brown was proud to be in United States Army, the finest military service of the greatest country in the world, a beacon for freedom, the leader of the New World Order. The Army was his life, a life that had so much more depth, meaning and importance than it did before. He was entrusted with the valuable task of shaping young men and women under his charge to destroy the enemy and wipe terrorism from the planet. The enemy was the low-life, stinking Arabs, those sand niggers, the little maggots who had strapped bombs to themselves and had blown his comrades to bits in Iraq. They were like a disease, a plague that had to be wiped out.

"I have the right to talk to an attorney," Ahmed pleaded.

"You what? You don't have any rights, A-hab," said Brown, "You're a terrorist. The only right you have is to choose to wear the mask or not, and you already exercised that right."

The young soldier fastened a leather strap around Ahmed's waist, pinning his spine to a wooden post. He turned his head to look behind himself at the canvas wall, pocked with gunshots. The soldier then strapped his ankles to the post.

"Please, let me call my lawyer. This is all a big mistake!"

"Yeah, yeah, a big mistake. I've heard that one before. All you fucking Hajis say the same goddamn thing – it's programmed. You should have cooperated when we asked about your superiors in al Qaeda."

"I don't know anyone in al Qaeda."

"Don't bullshit me, boy!"

Brown, like a machine, pivoted, walked a few paces, and then pivoted again, so he was face to face with Ahmed, took a piece of paper from his pocket, unfolded it and recited in a military monotone, "You have been found guilty of terrorism. The penalty is death by firing squad. Do you have any last statement?"

"But I…"

"I repeat, do you have any last statement?"

"Yes, please, I want to cooperate, I really do, but I don't know what you want from me. I don't know anything!"

The young man with the M16 then approached Ahmed, pinned a white heart onto his chest, and moved back. Brown marched off to the right of the firing squad.

Sweat was dripping into Ahmed's eyes, stinging them. He said a silent prayer, thought about his wife and children, then looked at Brown with defiant eyes.

"I'm not a terrorist. I am an American citizen. I have the right, like any other American citizen, to a lawyer and a trial before any execution. I have been denied these rights. You will answer to God for your crimes."

"To hell with your rights, boy. We got all the rights here," said Brown, who raised his arm and shouted, "READY!"

The eight marksmen cocked their rifles.

"AIM!"

The eight pointed their rifles at Ahmed, who shivered uncontrollably. His knees gave way and he hung on the post like a man crucified.

"FIRE!"

The deafening explosion of the eight rifles was the last thing Ahmed heard. He felt the bullets hit his flesh and his body crumpled forward, hanging lifelessly from the post like a scarecrow.

CHAPTER TWO

Catherine Khury sat in the plain-wrap waiting room of the FBI's Santa Barbara field office, fidgeting in her purse for her phone. *Hold it together, Cate!* she told herself. She had been living in hell the past few weeks. She was an attractive woman, but her ordeal made every one of her 30 years appear as if she had lived her life without sleeping. She looked at the time. Only five minutes had passed since the last time she had checked. A friendly looking, pretty young woman entered the room.

"Hello, ma'am, I'm Agent Wollard," the woman said, extending her hand, which Catherine shook.

"Catherine Khury."

"Would you please come in?"

Catherine sat in a small steel and vinyl black chair and Agent Wollard behind an aluminum desk with a false wood veneer surface.

"How can I help you, Mrs. Khury?"

"My husband, Ahmed, is missing." Catherine's bottom lip began to quiver, as she fought back tears. She had to remain strong; strong for her husband, and especially for her children.

"Mrs. Khury, we don't really look for missing persons here at the FBI."

"That's not what I heard."

"Well, we do maintain a database of missing persons, but unless it's a child, and foul play is suspected, we don't really get actively involved."

"Agent Wollard, I don't know where else to go. My husband and his brother have been missing since my husband went to Iraq to help him."

"Your husband is in Iraq?"

"The last I heard. But nobody has seen or heard from him in days," Catherine sobbed, struggling to keep her composure.

Angela handed her a tissue from the box on her desk. "Is your husband a United States citizen?"

"Yes, he has been for many years."

The tears finally made their way over the spillgates, and Catherine emptied them into the tissue.

"Have you tried to find him in Iraq?"

"Yes, but the only person I know there is his brother and he's not answering. I don't have anyone else to call."

"Well, the best I can do is to take a missing persons report and make a couple of phone calls."

"Would you please?" Catherine felt instant relief. Even though this Agent Wollard didn't promise a solution, just having any kind of help made her feel less hopeless.

"Yes, of course. Please, fill out these forms and, when you're done, I can enter the information into our missing person's database."

"Thank you Agent Wollard."

"I'm sorry I couldn't do more."

***

After Mrs. Khury left, Angela processed the report, and then called Bill Thompson, one of her contacts in Washington.

"Bill, I've got a missing person's case that I may need your help on."

"Since when does the bureau really ever work a missing person's case?"

Angela chuckled. "I've been known to do it from time to time. Listen, he's an Iraqi born, U.S. citizen, who went to Iraq last month and nobody has heard from him in about a week. His wife is worried to death."

"Send me an email and I'll make some calls."

"Thanks Bill."

CHAPTER THREE

Ahmed opened his eyes to complete blackness. *Am I alive?* Panicking, he put his hand in front of his face and he couldn't see it. He moved his fingers. Still nothing. Ahmed's frantic eyes moved back and forth and there was not a sliver of light. *I'm blind,* he thought. A sudden surge of adrenalin compelled him to action. His brain sent a signal to stand up and, as he did, the pain shot from his feet to his head like a hammer hit on a high striker in a carnival. Gravity pulled his broken body to his knees and he collapsed. He felt his body: No clothing.

What happened? Am I dead?

No, he thought, *I must be alive*. He was in too much pain to be dead. He felt his chest for bullet wounds, but found none. Except for some tender spots on his chest and back and some scrapes on his knees, there was nothing. *They must have used rubber bullets.*

Ahmed strained to see, but it was no use. He felt his face: It was swollen and bruised. *They must have blinded me in the shooting,* he thought. As his other four senses came to life, he realized that he was sore all over. He tried to stand again, but his legs would not cooperate. He felt them with his new eyes; the bones felt straight and unbroken. *Must be sprains, but why am I blind?* He struggled to control the panic and the terror. *Think, think. Have to think.*

Ahmed crawled on his hands and knees and propped himself up against the wall, which was as cold and damp as the floor. He felt along the walled boundaries of his confinement. *One, two, three, four, five, six, about seven feet in one direction. One, two, three, four, about five feet in the other direction.* Next, he negotiated the circumference on his hands and knees.

How did he get himself into this mess? From his cozy home in Santa Barbara, to the battered and occupied Baghdad, to this. His brother, Sabeen needed his help, so he went. It was as simple as that. The next events were a blur to him; The raid, his capture. Now he was in some kind of military prison.

Since his capture, Ahmed had been stripped naked, cavity searched, shaved bald, beaten, kicked and spat on. And then the mock execution. It made his current confinement in this dark cage somewhat of a relief, not at all what it was designed for. The walls were as cold as a headstone. He felt around them until he came to a steel door.

He thought of his wife, Catherine. She must know he was missing by now. But even if he was to be rescued, what good is a blind husband? An accountant by trade, there was no way he could work with figures as a blind man. He would be a complete burden on the entire family. *The best thing to do is to kill myself,* he thought. He had some life insurance, and wondered if it would pay off in the event of his suicide.

***

The time passed, but Ahmed had no way of measuring it. *How long have I been like this?* Ahmed concentrated on his other senses, but there was no input, save the sound of the pounding of his own heart. His mouth was as dry as a slab of jerky, so he tried to wet his broken lips with his tongue. In despair, he dropped to the floor. Lying there on his back, he

13

rubbed his eyes and, suddenly, he saw tiny stars above him in the blackness. *Light! I can see light!*

The tiny stars spread out in a geometric pattern, like symbols in a matrix. *Those can't be stars. They're not random.* Ahmed's accountant's brain analyzed the patterns of light, but then they turned into eyes, angrily staring at him. *Stop! Stop! Please, somebody help me!* Then the eyes pulled back to reveal a miniature firing squad, with their rifles trained on Ahmed. He heard the blast of their rifles, almost in slow motion, and felt the bullets ripping through his flesh as his brain switched off.

CHAPTER FOUR

Ahmed opened his eyes to complete darkness again. He was still blind, but the need to urinate affirmed that he was still alive.

His nostrils filled with the sweet smell of food: chicken…thyme…rosemary…potatoes. *Soup!*

But was it real? On his hands and knees, he crawled the surface of the concrete floor, looking for the soup and for something to pee in, just in case he had to drink his own urine to survive. If worse came to worse, he could eat the soup and then pee in the container.

Gingerly, his hands methodically covered the surface of the floor, until they met resistance. Gripping it with his fingers, he realized it was a Styrofoam cup, about 12 ounces in capacity. He explored inside, the cup with one finger. *Water!* But Ahmed resisted the impulse to drain the cup. Instead he smelled it, and, sensing no foul odor, tasted just a bit on his tongue. It was fresh and cooling, which immediately gave rise to the instinctual urge to gulp it down. Not wanting to throw it up, Ahmed took a mouthful and swirled it around with his tongue before swallowing. The taste of minerals and the cool wetness was the most pleasing thing he had experienced in such a long time. Ahmed slowly savored every drop of the precious water, and then continued on his quest refreshed.

***

The soup was still lukewarm when Ahmed found it. He grasped the small bowl with both hands as the aroma filled his lungs, and sipped on the broth, then reached in and pulled out a piece of potato. It was the best thing he had ever tasted.

There was no telling how long his stomach had been empty. The pangs of hunger had subsided long ago and, since he had no way of tracking time, that concept had fallen away from his consciousness, as the hunger had. Ahmed knew that this first taste of food in who knows how long may be his last for a while, so he saved half the bowl for later, knowing that the hunger would return as soon as his body realized it had been nourished once again.

He had only spent a few days with Sabeen before the military police took them away and separated them. *Sabeen was a grocer! Why would they think he was a terrorist?* Since then, Ahmed had lived the nightmare of his new life in captivity, first aboard a military transport, then on a huge jet, all the while with bound hands and feet and a hood over his head, until he was dumped on the ground, naked, in this new prison, wherever it was. He couldn't remember the last time he had eaten before such delicious chicken soup.

CHAPTER FIVE

Angela put on her sweater and looked at herself in her pocket mirror. She wiped off a bit of the stray mascara around her green eyes and put a brush through her hair. Just as she was about to lock up the office, the phone rang.

"Agent Wollard," she answered.

"Angie, it's Bill. I've got some info on your Mr. Khury, but it's not something you want to get involved in."

"I'll decide that Bill, what've you got?"

"Khury shows up in Baghdad about three weeks ago. His brother, Sabeen, is a suspected money launderer for al Qaeda."

"I see. CIA talk." The CIA was always looking to tie every kind of criminal activity in the Middle East to al Qaeda.

"You got that right."

"Since when does the CIA tell the Bureau what to do?"

"Since we have no jurisdiction. Khury's in Guantanamo."

"That shit hole is still open?"

"Damn right it is. Please, don't tell anyone I told you, and for God's sake, don't get involved. This is classified stuff."

"Who says?"

"It comes from high up."

"How high?"

"Lose your job high, get it?"

"I do Bill, thanks."

"We're square now, Angie, this was a big one."

***

"You're late again." Rick Penn stood up and smiled, his six foot six inch frame towering over the small table as Angela nervously paced into the restaurant. Rick was a retired FBI agent, now a private investigator, and had been Angela's mentor during her first days in the bureau. At 54, he had served out his last days with the Bureau in Santa Barbara, and then retired there. Now he could take it easy and be his own boss. For years, Rick had worn the same type of G-man suit, but now he was free of those chains and could wear whatever he pleased. But, for his meeting with Angela today, he dressed up in a white shirt, tie and baggy pants: The Columbo look.

"I'm sorry, it's my job."

"I know. All is forgiven. They saved us the best table."

The maître d' led them to a nice table in front of a crackling fireplace. Santa Barbara had many cozy restaurants like Cava. Nestled on Coast Village Road in Montecito, having a meal there was comfy, like being in your own living room.

"Rick, I know somebody who needs your help, but I could lose my job for telling you about it."

"You could always join my PI firm, retire early like me," Rick smiled, "Now tell me about this potential client?"

"He's a naturalized citizen, being held at Guantanamo."

"Guano-mo, huh? The neo-Nazi concentration camp."

"Yes. His wife came to me to file a missing person's case. I think you should talk to her."

Rick brushed his graying hair out of his eyes. "You're a few weeks shy of a haircut, aren't you Rick?"

Rick chuckled. "At least I have some hair left. Just email me her contact info and I'll give her a call."

"Thanks Rick."

Rick had read a lot about the suspected terrorists being held at Guantanamo Bay indefinitely. It was the kind of case that Rick's best friend, lawyer Brent Marks, had always dreamed about: Going against the grain to fight for an individual's rights. After 18 years of slugging it out as a "poor man's lawyer" Brent had gained plenty of experience righting wrongs, but there was only so much you could do with a drunk driving or spousal abuse case. This case sounded like fertile Constitutional Law ground for Brent, and Rick would keep the investigation gig on the case.

The military prison at Guantanamo was the equivalent of any concentration camp in Nazi Germany, the most shameful example of the cruel and complete abolition of all human rights by the Government, all in the name of the war on terrorism. Two days after the September 11th attacks, the Congress gave authority to the president to use military force, and, since then, the military, not the U.S. courts, had jurisdiction over anyone suspected as an "enemy combatant," And could do with them as they pleased, without the constraints of the U.S. Constitution.

CHAPTER SIX

Rick called Brent and arranged to meet later that day after work. That could be a somewhat vague term for Brent, who was quite the workaholic when he was on a case. They had met about eight years earlier, when Rick had walked into Brent's office and scared the crap out of him by flashing his FBI badge. It turned out Rick was just looking for some legal advice for a case he was working on. The two stayed in contact and became close over the years.

Brent was wrapping up an interview with a potential client, an Indian guy who had been accused of a hit and run, not the type of a case he had been dreaming of, but the kind he had been known to take to keep the doors open. The client was trying to explain his case to Brent, but it seemed he didn't have much of a defense.

"I'm having a little trouble following your story, Mr. Babu. You're telling me that you hit the car, and you didn't stop, right?"

"No, no, that's not it at all. I hit the guy, and then I look around, and I don't see him. Then I drive around and around and around, and I still do not see the guy, so I go home."

"So you didn't stop?"

"How could I stop when I did not see the guy?"

"Mr. Babu, if I take your case, I'm going to require a retainer up front."

"But I don't have any cash. Look, look, my cousin is a tailor in Hong Kong. He makes the best suits in the world. Do you need a suit?"

"You want to pay me in suits?"

"Yes, please, look, look, I have the swatches right here." Babu pulled some material samples from his bag, and held them out to Brent. "Feel the material. It is the finest material in the world!"

"I don't know, Mr. Babu."

"Please, Mr. Marks. You must take my case. I will pay you in suits now, and then, when I get some money, I will give you money. You must help me. I cannot sleep, I cannot make

26

love with my wife. It is like a death in the family!"

It was almost a comedy. Brent felt the urge to look around the room for the hidden camera. He suppressed a grin.

"It's late, Mr. Babu. Can I call you tomorrow with my decision?"

"Yes, yes, thank you Mr. Marks, thank you!"

***

Brent closed up the office and left. With 18 years of practice under his belt, he was close to being able to decline the Mr. Babus and focus on more important cases. He thought of the comical interview and laughed to himself. Brent was the first American of his generation, so he had a soft spot for the immigrants.

His father, Jose, had emigrated from Spain and completely assimilated into American pop culture, even changed the family name from Marquez to Marks. Thankfully, his father spoke Spanish at home to Brent and his brother John. It was an advantage that came in handy in the practice of his profession.

27

At about seven, Brent walked into the Press Room on Ortega Street to find his friend Rick waiting at the bar.

"There he is! What's up, Big Dog?"

"Hey, Rick."

Rick rose from the bar stool, so tall a man that it seemed he would hit the ceiling, and swung into a power handshake with Brent.

"Good to see you, buddy," said Rick.

"You too. It's been a long time." Brent slid into the chair next to Rick at the sticky bar counter.

"Dude, you're supposed to be a bachelor. Only married men have your dead boring social life."

"Yeah, well I've kind of been seeing somebody."

"Do tell. Come on, give me all the details, and don't leave out the measurements. 36-24-36, D cup?"

"Come on, man!"

"No, dude, I'm happy for you whenever you have a relationship that lasts more than three weeks. It's not that piece of ass secretary of yours – Melinda – is it?"

"No, no, her name is Debbie."

"Debbie? As in dumb blonde Debbie Does Dallas, something like that?"

"Dude! It's not like that. I'm really enjoying her company."

"So, a meaningful relationship. Dude, have fun, but wear a condom, that's all I can say."

"Very funny. What's this new case that you've taken on?"

"Really interesting. And it's your kind of case. Not one of those nut jobs you take to pay the rent."

"I've still got a few of those."

"I know, but this one is really juicy. This rag head marries an American girl, right? He's the gung-ho, I love America kind of immigrant, accountant, two kids, the house, the whole nine yards. Becomes a U.S. citizen…"

"Yeah?"

"Then his brother calls him with some kind of family crisis back in Iraq, and he goes, right? Well, his brother is involved in some kind of money laundering operation back there – he's got this cash grocery business – and he gets raided by MPs. Our guy gets picked up and shipped to Gitmo."

Brent almost choked on his beer. "What?"

"That's right. They're keeping him there; think he's some kind of terrorist. No charges, no counsel, no visitors. A virtual Nazi prison camp."

"Whoa, watch it. I thought you were a flag-waving Republican."

"Dude, this transcends politics. George W. Bush is wiping his ass with the Constitution."

"Careful, that's your ex-boss you're talking about."

"Yeah, the same one who said to the Brazilian president, 'Oh do you have blacks too?'" Rick snorted and took a gulp of beer.

"How about, 'Africa is a nation that suffers from incredible disease,'" said Brent, wiping away tears he was laughing so hard.

"It would be funny if it wasn't so tragic." Rick gargled his beer between laughs.

"My favorite one is, 'this foreign policy stuff is a little frustrating.' Like he's learning it in high school or something."

"How about, 'I know what I believe. I will continue to articulate what I believe and what I believe. I believe what I believe is right.' It's almost enough to make me turn into a Democrat, like you."

"Dude, I'm not a Democrat, I'm a Libertarian."

"A Libertarian's just a Democrat whose vote doesn't count. Same thing."

"How'd you find out about this case anyway?" asked Brent, trying to get back on a serious track.

"Dude, I'm a secret agent man."

"From someone in the Bureau."

"Exactly, a confidential source. Look, I've talked to his wife and I recommended you for the job."

Rick was right. Brent was so enthusiastic about the case he had to practically fight him not to go back to the office.

"I can't wait to take this case, Rick."

"Dude, chill out. It'll still be there in the morning. I'm not letting anyone else have it."

CHAPTER SEVEN

Brent's secretary Melinda announced Catherine Khury. Brent walked into the office waiting room to greet her and show her in.

Mrs. Khury was not what Brent had expected. She was American, of obvious European descent, about 30 years old, with light brown hair and eyes. She seemed a little shy and more than a bit nervous.

"Brent Marks," he said, extending his hand.

She took it. Her hand was warm and pleasant, but the handshake was shaky. "Catherine Khury."

"Please have a seat."

Catherine sat down in one of the two classic wooden, unpadded chairs across from Brent's desk. It was designed to encourage a visit of the required length only.

"Mrs. Khury, as I told you on the phone, I am interested in helping you with your husband's matter," said Brent.

"I'm so thankful your investigator Mr. Penn found him, but I can't believe he's being held as a suspected terrorist. How can I see him?" Katherine asked, fidgeting with her purse on her lap.

"Actually, Mrs. Khury, I didn't find him; he was located by a confidential source who asked me to reveal the information to you. And, as far as being able to see him, I'm not sure the Government will allow that yet."

"Why not? Ahmed's a good man. He never had anything to do with terrorists."

"I believe you, but they haven't even acknowledged that they have him."

"What do we do?" Catherine started to cry. "It seems to be impossible."

"Of course, you have no obligation to hire me, but what you could do is file a petition for a writ of *habeas corpus* in Federal Court here in the States. If that's granted, he will have a hearing in a U.S. Court on U.S. soil instead of being held indefinitely in Cuba."

"Indefinitely?"

"Yes, some suspected terrorists have been there since 2003. If they are accused of being 'enemy combatants' they can be held as long as it is deemed fit, without a trial. But they do have a right to challenge whether they are enemy combatants or not."

"Ahmed is not an enemy of the United States. He loves America. And he's not a terrorist!"

"The Government thinks he is, and they think that gives them the ability to foreclose all his rights."

"Is this expensive, this *habeas corpus*?"

"Yes, it is. I can give you a very good hourly rate, but I can't work for free. We'll be fighting the Government, and they'll throw everything at us to crush our petition. It's going to take a lot of hours."

"I'll do whatever it takes to save Ahmed. I've got some savings, and I'll borrow money if I have to."

"I'll see if I can get the Government to admit they have him, and the next step will be to go down there to talk to him."

"I'll go with you."

"Let me see what I can do first, then we'll try to set up visitation for you, okay?"

"You're my last hope, Mr. Marks. I've tried everything and every door closes in my face. The only ones who even tried to help me were that FBI agent and Mr. Penn.

Brent was accustomed to the way tribal bias and prejudice gave way to mistreatment in his native America, his Hispanic looks being mistaken for Mexican more than once.

Brent left Catherine with the assignment of digging up every piece of paper she could on Ahmed: a copy of his passport, his naturalization papers, his work history, even his banking records.

Brent would have to present on paper the picture of a good American citizen. George W. Bush said, "It will take time to restore chaos." Brent was about to confront Bush's creation head on.

CHAPTER EIGHT

Ahmed's tortured soul finally got to rest, but it wasn't for long. In the middle of the night his tormented sleep was interrupted by a strong hand over his nose and mouth. Ahmed swung his panicked arms, which were caught by another strong pair of hands, which restrained him as his ears were muffed and his head was bagged with some type of hood device. *Am I dreaming?* he thought.

Unfortunately, it was no dream. Ahmed was still blind, but his heightened senses of smell and hearing could not help him. The hood and ear muffs deprived him of both. As the two men took turns pushing him along, once again he had the sensation of falling in space, only to be broken by the reality of the hard ground. Ahmed struggled to get up, to the laughter of his captors.

The two men shoved Ahmed into a room and pushed him down onto a flat, cold surface. He felt them immobilize and strap his arms and legs with some kind of restraints. Then, as the hood and ear muffs were ripped from his head, the room exploded with brilliant white light and a symphony of sounds. His eyes stung. *I'm not blind!* He moved his head from side to side, as blurry images came into focus. *What's happening?* But just as he experienced that realization which should have given him tremendous happiness, his torturers confronted him, once again.

"Now you're gonna tell us, Haji, what you were doing in Baghdad," said a grinning Sergeant Brown.

"My name is not Haji."

"Shut up! Everyone's a Haji here," screamed Brown, an inch from Ahmed's face. He could feel the spit from his lips and smell his stale tobacco breath.

"You fucking maggots are all the same, and, if it was up to me, I would squash every last one of you!"

Brown moved back, and two suited strangers moved in. Their lack of military garb and their stoic expressions set them apart from the rest of the robots in camouflage gear. One threw a cloth over Ahmed's face.

"What were you doing in Baghdad?" asked one of the strangers.

"I went to see my brother, he needed my help."

"You helped your brother with his money laundering operation?"

"What? No. He's a grocer. He said he was in trouble. I came to do whatever I could to help him."

"So you helped him launder money for al Qaeda. Who did you meet there from al Qaeda?"

"I don't know anyone from al Qaeda!"

"I'm going to ask you one more time. Who did you meet from al Qaeda? I want names."

"I didn't…"

Ahmed gasped for air as water was poured on the cloth over his face. He felt like he was drowning, as one of the men poured water into the cloth. He gasped for air, but all he felt was water in his nose and mouth. It was impossible to breathe, so he held his breath.

After what seemed like a lifetime, the cloth was lifted and Ahmed sucked in and blew out air one, two…three times, then they slapped the cloth back on his face and he was drowning again.

"You went to Baghdad to help your brother launder money, didn't you?"

The cloth came off, and Ahmed sucked in air, as if he had reached the surface of the water.

"No! He needed my help!"

They again slapped the wet cloth over Ahmed's face and poured water over it. Ahmed held his breath for what seemed like the longest time. *This is it*, he thought. *If I stop holding my breath, I die.*

CHAPTER NINE

After an eternity, Ahmed was moved from solitary confinement to a concrete block cell, with concrete walls, a solid steel door with no bars and no windows, about ten feet long, seven feet wide and about eight feet high. Unlike his solitary cell, it had a stainless steel wash basin/toilet combination, and a part of the wall was fashioned into a bed with a thin mattress and a pillow. Bright light blazed through the wire mesh ceiling, accompanied by loud, heavy metal music.

It was difficult for Ahmed to get used to the routine because it varied. At any given moment, he was rousted from his cell for further interrogation, which was always preceded by a rectal and groin search. Following the questioning, he was either forced to stand for eight hours, or forced to crawl inside a small metal box and stay there for four hours. The standing was easier.

*＊＊

No sooner than Ahmed had accepted his fate, and drifted to sleep, he was awakened by four soldiers in full riot gear, his head covered in a sensory deprivation mask, and taken out of his cell. As the men led him away from his cell, they body slammed him into the walls as they moved him along to the interrogation room, where he was left, masked and shackled, until he had lost all track of time. Ahmed figured it was approximately nine hours, but he had no point of reference.

When the mask was finally taken off, Ahmed got a chance to breathe, but not for long. As he lay on the floor, he looked up and saw the two suits who had waterboarded him.

"Hello again," said one of the suits.

"What do you want from me? I told you everything," said a terrified Ahmed.

"We just want to make sure you didn't leave out any details," said the suit.

Ahmed's hands and feet were shackled to a solid steel chair, which was bolted to the ground. Then, one of the agents stuffed some rags in his mouth and said, "Listen very carefully, your life depends on it."

The agent peeled off a generous section of duct tape, ripped it off with his teeth and, to Ahmed's horror, taped it over his nose and mouth. In a panic, Ahmed writhed and buckled against his constraints. His body craved air, and his faced turned blue. He felt faint, like he was going to pass out, and thought, *this is the end.* In his mind, he said goodbye to his darling Catherine, Cameron and Karen, and their faces flashed before his eyes.

Then, the agent ripped the tape off, and, like a drowning man reaching the surface of the water Ahmed gulped in as much air as he could.

"Now we want the details," the agent said, as he removed the rags from Ahmed's mouth while the other agent looked on.

"What details?"

To that, the agent had no verbal response. He simply stuffed the rags back into Ahmed's mouth. All of Ahmed's movements to resist were as futile as an insect trying to escape the crushing heel of a boot. *Why don't they just kill me?* he thought, *Put me out of everyone's misery.*

43

CHAPTER TEN

Sergeant Brown marched into his CO's office, stood in front of his desk and saluted.

"At ease, Sergeant," said Colonel Masters, who busied himself with reports on his desk. Masters was a career officer, on his last tour of duty before retirement. He had no love for anyone, and even less patience. He looked up at Brown with an empty expression. "A civilian lawyer from California is coming today to visit one of your Hajis."

"Which Haji is that sir?"

"Khury."

"He's a troublemaker, sir. Doesn't want to talk. The spooks were at him all day yesterday."

"Just make sure the lawyer is comfortable, and that he understands all the rules."

"Yes, sir."

Masters went back to his reading, paused, and then looked up. Brown was still there, waiting to be dismissed.

"That'll be all, Sergeant."

"Yes, Sir." Brown saluted, turned and walked out the door.

✳✳✳

"Welcome to Guantanamo Bay," said the pilot over the PA system as the small plane kissed the tarmac. Brent looked outside the window: Not very welcoming at all. It looked as he had expected; military buildings of sorts installed on hills in a chaparral type landscape.

As he exited the plane, a heavy wall of sticky tropical heat filled his lungs and, by the time he reached the bottom of the stairs, he was already wiping beads of sweat from his forehead.

After being processed, Brent was given a military clearance pass marked "Escort Only" to get him onto the base. He was assigned Corporal Reeding, a 20-year-old soldier from Macon, Georgia, as his escort. Brent supposed that Reeding would be at his side to make sure he didn't see anything he wasn't supposed to see, or talk to anyone he wasn't supposed to talk to. The two of them boarded a ferry to cross the bay to the windward side of the island.

Reeding could have been any kid in any American town, attending the University, cheating on his studies during the week and getting drunk every weekend. In his military camouflage fatigues, he looked as out of place as a little boy trying on his father's suit.

"So you're a civilian lawyer, sir?" asked Reeding.

"Yes, why?"

"We don't get too many civilian lawyers here. Mostly military lawyers or lawyers appointed by the Pentagon."

"I see."

"After the ferry, we're going to be transported to Camp 7," said Reeding.

"I hear they call it 'Camp No' because if anyone asks about it, they say it doesn't exist."

"I wouldn't know about that, sir."

When the ferry docked, Reeding escorted Brent to a khaki-colored van with no windows in the back or sides.

"This is our transport, sir. Before we get out, you'll have to choose which one of these blindfold devices to wear."

Reeding help up a regular looking blindfold in one hand, and a black hood that seemed like it would cover the entire head."

"Which one do the detainees wear?"

"They're required to wear the hood, sir."

"I'll take the hood."

The inside of the van was a windowless box. Brent could not even see into the driver's compartment. Reeding rode in the back with Brent, as they took a seemingly circuitous route over the bumpy terrain, and, finally, came to a stop. The cloak and dagger security was almost ridiculous. To get on the base required military clearance. To get to the prison required even more red tape. Reeding handed Brent the hood, he put it on, and Reeding adjusted it. Brent heard the van door open and felt the tropical heat again instantly. Reeding helped him out of the van. Inside the hood it was completely black and it didn't take long before it became hot and very uncomfortable.

"You okay, sir?" asked Reeding.

"Yes, but it's kind of uncomfortable with this hood. How much longer do I have to wear it?"

"Not too much longer, sir. Don't worry."

Brent heard the sound of the metallic chain link gates being opened and closed, and finally the clang of a metal door, as Reeding guided him into the prison camp.

When Reeding lifted the hood, Brent found himself inside a concrete compound. Several military personnel, male and female, in camouflage fatigues moved about busily. Brent was asked to take off his watch, his belt, to empty his pockets, and put his briefcase through the X-ray machine before going through the metal detector.

"Sir, may I open your briefcase?" said the X-ray screener.

"Yes, of course."

The screener looked through the pockets of the briefcase, pulling out Brent's legal pad, pens, and a sealed envelope.

"What's in the envelope, sir?"

"It's a letter to my client from his wife.

The screener took the letter and the briefcase, and handed the pad and one pen back to Brent.

"You'll get the rest of the materials back when you leave."

"What about the letter?"

"It'll be put through secondary screening."

"What for?" Brent asked.

Reeding answered, "Some al Qaeda operatives have been known to receive terrorist communications from their relatives. I'll escort you to the conference area," said Reeding, and Brent followed him down the corridor.

Once inside the conference area, which was a windowless room, Brent sat on a small stool that protruded from a metal arm, welded to a solid steel table, and looked around at the four blank concrete walls as he waited for his client. He noticed not one, but two smoke alarms in the ceiling, which he surmised were equipped with video and audio devices, because the "test buttons" were clear and seemed to be pointed at the conference table.

"Can I be assured that my meeting with my client will be confidential?" he asked Reeding.

"Sir, all the attorneys have the opportunity to discuss matters confidentially with their clients," he answered.

Suddenly, not his client, but another soldier, entered the room and closed the door.

"Hello sir, my name is Sergeant Brown," he said. Sergeant Brown, like the rest of the soldiers he had seen, wore camouflage fatigues and looked very serious. He was a towering black man with very big hands that looked as if he could tear you apart with them. Brent thought, *this is never someone you would want to meet in a dark alley.*

"Hello Sergeant."

"I just want to remind you of the rules here, sir. It is prohibited to discuss the facilities of Camp 7 with anyone from outside this camp. Do you understand?"

"Yes."

"And it is prohibited to discuss your client's jihadist activities, do you understand?"

"He has no jihadist activities."

"Sir, I asked, do you understand?"

"Yes, I understand."

"It is prohibited to discuss with your client information about current or former detention personnel, do you understand?"

"Yes."

"And you must speak in the same language to your client, do you understand?"

"Is English alright, Sergeant?"

Brown scowled at Brent. "Do you understand, sir?"

"Yes, I understand. Sergeant, may I ask you a question?"

"What, sir?"

"What can I speak with my client about?"

"Sir, I am only explaining the rules about attorney-client communications in Camp 7. I am not restricting your attorney-client communications. Do I have your agreement that you will abide by these rules?"

"Well I don't have much choice do I?"

"Do I have your agreement, sir?"

"Yes, you have my agreement. Will my conversation with my client be monitored, Sergeant?"

"Sir, I cannot discuss any more details with you. My objective is simply to determine that you will comply with the rules."

"I will comply."

Sergeant Brown handed Brent the envelope containing the letter from Ahmed's wife. It had been opened. "Your letter has been cleared for the detainee," he said.

When we deny the rights of others, we deny them to ourselves. Brent felt ashamed that his country, once a leader in human rights, had gone down this sorry path, sacrificing personal rights for an illusion of safety.

CHAPTER ELEVEN

Brown brought in Ahmed, hooded and shackled and dressed in an orange jump suit. He put him in his seat, fastened his ankle shackles to one of the fixed metal posts of Ahmed's chair, and his hands to a post on the table.

"Is that really necessary?" asked Brent.

"Sir, do I have to remind you that this is a classified facility, with strict procedures, and that you are here as our guest? A guest who has agreed to abide by those procedures?"

"No, you don't. Now, may I have a confidential discussion with my client?"

Brown removed Ahmed's hood and turned for the door. "You have fifteen minutes," he said as he walked away.

"Wait a minute!"

Brown shut the door. Brent stood up and looked at the smoke detector with the lens pointed at his side of the table, and spoke directly to it. "Nobody told me that our time would be limited. I need more than fifteen minutes with my client to prepare our case! And, for the record, we do not agree to a surveillance of this conversation. It is a privileged attorney-client communication."

He turned his attention back to the shackled man at the table. Ahmed looked tired, worn down and emaciated, like he hadn't eaten or slept for days. But, even so, he had a pleasant and friendly look. He didn't fit Brent's preconceived image of what a terrorist would look like. He looked simply like one of the many Muslim immigrants Brent had seen: doctors, taxi drivers, lawyers and accountants; his experience with them had never been negative.

"Ahmed, my name is Brent Marks. Your wife hired me to be your attorney."

"Hello Mr. Marks," said Ahmed. "I would shake your hand but, as you can see, my hands are handcuffed to this table." Ahmed gestured with his hands within the limitations of their restraints. "And they don't allow any personal contact."

"Yes, I've noticed there are many differences here than prisons in the United States."

"Oh, but Mr. Marks, this is not a prison."

"So I heard. Now, I'm not allowed to ask you about any of your jihadist activities."

"I don't have any jihadist activities!" Ahmed's forehead wrinkled in frustration and he looked defeated. All he could think about was how he had just met this lawyer, and the lawyer had preconceived notions that he was some kind of a terrorist.

"I know. But there are certain things I'm not allowed to speak to you about and to represent you, I had to be clear on your status. Now I am."

"I'm not a terrorist, Mr. Marks. I'm just a U.S. citizen who was born in Iraq. I love my life in America and my new country."

"Why did you go to Baghdad?"

"I got a call from my brother. He said he needed my help."

"With what?"

"He couldn't say. But I could tell he was in trouble."

"So you went to Iraq, knowing that your brother was in some kind of trouble, but you didn't ask what?"

"He's my brother! He asks for help, I go. It's that simple."

"And what happened after your arrival?"

"That's just it. Nothing happened! My brother picked me up at the airport, drove me to his place, and I spent a few days there. Before he had a chance to tell me what was wrong and how I could help, there was a raid."

"A raid?"

"Yes. One of my brother's friends got a call, and they all left: they went out the window. A few minutes later, the MP's were breaking down his door."

"What happened to your brother?"

"I don't know. They separated us. I think they killed him." Ahmed hung his head in despair.

"Ahmed, I don't know how much time we really have."

"He said fifteen minutes…"

"Yes, so let's use all of the time we have wisely."

Brent jotted down everything that Ahmed could remember, about his brother, the names of his friends, and every detail about his time in Iraq.

"So your brother runs a store. That's why they suspected him of being a money launderer."

"Yes, but that little store couldn't possibly take in that much cash."

"Ahmed, I'm going to file a procedure called a habeas corpus in Federal Court in the States. If the application is granted, you can be moved to the States and get a trial there."

"I don't even know what they're charging me with. They won't say."

"You leave that to me."

***

Ahmed recounted a tale of torture and abuse that rivaled that of Nazi Germany or the Spanish Inquisition. He described the isolation of the concrete holding cells with no windows and steel doors instead of bars, to prevent contact among inmates. He told of fellow inmates' suicides and the famous force-feeding chair, for those who attempted hunger strikes. In short, his story violated every parameter that Brent was given for the interview, but the explosive facts made a habeas corpus petition a virtual shoe-in.

There was a pounding on the door and Brown entered. "Time's up," he declared.

Brent handed Ahmed the letter from his wife.

"From your wife."

Ahmed took the letter with his shackled hands and looked at it in awe as if it was a bar of gold. His eyes, filled with gratitude, met Brent's. He smiled as opened it and read, *My dearest love, It has been so long since I wrote a letter to you. Pressures and responsibilities of life can make some things seem routine, but it's always a happiness to be by your side, sharing everything together. I feel so lost without you; like I'm drifting aimlessly in the darkness of space. There is always quiet peace at the end of the day, after the children have gone to bed and we spend time together just being with each other. It's always been my favorite time. But now it's just a quiet time; quiet and empty and the peace is gone. I miss your warm touch, your gentle strength; that security I feel in your presence. I miss waking up with you by my side and falling to sleep at night on your shoulder. It seems I can't sleep without it.*

I can't imagine the terrible ordeal that you are going through, and I feel selfish when I wallow here in my own misery. But I know that we will be together soon, so that gives me hope. I pray every day that this will be the day you come home. Know always that my heart is always full of love for you. Karen and Cameron are sending you their hugs and kisses. I haven't told them what's going on yet. They still think you're in Iraq...

Brown tore the letter from Ahmed's handcuffed hand and bagged his head. "The interview is over," he declared.

It was William Penn who said, "Right is right, even if everyone is against it, and wrong is wrong, even if everyone is for it." Brent knew that there was nothing right about this place and the way the prisoners were treated, and he was determined to do whatever he could to change that.

CHAPTER TWELVE

Brent's mind was working non-stop like a locomotive on the flight back to Los Angeles. When the plane landed in Miami, his first stop, everyone had to go through customs and immigration control. Brent knew that, but what was unusual was that the Captain had announced that every passenger should have passports out and ready to show them to officers as they deplaned.

It took unusually long for the plane to empty, and, when Brent reached the end of the jetway, there were two armed border patrol officers there checking passports. Brent showed his passport to them.

"Just the gentleman we've been looking for. Please come with us, sir."

One of the officers, a young man, took Brent by the arm, and the three men moved in tandem.

"What's this about?" asked Brent.

"We don't know. You'll have to discuss it with the interrogating officer," said the unattached officer.

"Am I being arrested?"

"Not at this time, sir," said the officer.

"Well then, why the armed escort?"

"Do you have an outstanding warrant for your arrest in any state?"

"No."

"Then, it's probably just routine."

Brent imagined a routine where long-term American citizens like him were treated like criminals every time they came back from a trip abroad. The walk to the screening section seemed like it would take forever. Brent had never been detained or placed in custody before. Sure, he had been in plenty of prisons, but never as the prisoner, only as a visitor.

The subsequent two-hour wait in the screening section, a locked area, with officers standing behind a glass wall like bank tellers, seemed like a lifetime.

"Excuse me, can you tell me how long this will take? I'm going to miss my connecting flight," he said to one teller.

"Wait for your name to be called," was the only response he was given.

They had retrieved Brent's name in-flight from the passenger list, which was automatically transmitted to the Department of Homeland Security in Miami. Someone had put an alert out for Brent's passport.

"Brent Marks," called one of the tellers.

Brent was shown into a private screening room, where an armed Border Patrol Officer sat in front of a computer.

"Mr. Marks, was this your first visit to Cuba?"

"Yes, but I didn't go to Cuba, technically it was Guantanamo Bay. That's considered U.S. territory."

"Are you trying to argue with a United States Border Patrol Officer, Sir?"

"No, I'm not, I just…"

"What was the purpose of your visit to Cuba?"

"I'm a lawyer. I was visiting a client."

"Can you prove that you're a lawyer?"

"Of course. Here's my bar card," Brent said, as he opened his wallet at took out his California State bar membership card.

"What is your final destination in the United States, sir?"

"Los Angeles."

After taking Brent's address, the name of his client, and examining the papers that proved he had been granted permission to visit Gitmo, the Officer said, "You're free to go, Mr. Marks. Welcome home."

"That's it?"

"Yes."

"What is this all about?"

"I'm afraid I cannot discuss that with you, Sir. If you have any questions or grievances, you can visit our website."

Welcome home. Brent had left the United States a free man. Why did he not feel free when he came back?

CHAPTER THIRTEEN

The long ride to Santa Barbara gave Brent pause to reflect on everything that had happened at Gitmo and his return. Now the surreal images of hooded and shackled prisoners in orange jumpsuits kneeling on the ground among armed guards that he had seen in news reports were a sobering reality. Something had to be done, and he was in a position to do it.

When he finally reached Coast Village Road, he exited the freeway and took the long way home by the beach. Brent had seen enough concrete on his trip to Gitmo, and he wanted to enjoy the fresh air and the lovely beach vista on the final few miles of the drive home.

Brent rolled down the windows and smelled the misty, salty air as he gazed across the palm studded grassy knolls of Chase Palm Park and its late afternoon joggers along Cabrillo Blvd. Once again, he was reminded why he chose Santa Barbara. L.A. had some nice spots, and it was great to be in the action, but it was a concrete jungle compared to Santa Barbara, which was calm and beautiful 365 days a year. Passing State Street, he saw people strolling along the beach among the bicycle riders and roller skaters on the bike path, and the tourists taking their walks down State Street to Stearns Wharf, perhaps to select a restaurant for the evening. Brent headed toward the Mesa via Shoreline Drive. The picture postcard view of the Santa Barbara harbor loomed above the houses as he descended toward his Harbor Hills Lane home.

When he walked in, he received a homecoming from his orange and white cat, Calico. Her cheerful face was always synonymous with home. Calico's purr motor was idling, and she rubbed her body against his legs, first with her face, and continuing along the length of her slinky body until the tip of her snaky tail. Then she repeated the process on the other leg, all the while idling at 700 rpm.

Before Brent had a chance to set down his suitcases to feed the cat, the phone rang. Brent set down his bags, negotiated what little space was left between them and the cat in the entry, and raced the cat to the kitchen to pick up the phone.

"Brent, it's Debbie, are you okay?"

"Hi, Deb, yes, I'm fine."

"I was just worried, haven't heard from you since I got your text that you landed. How did it go at Gitmo?"

"We should talk about it over dinner."

"Sounds good."

"Let me just jump in the shower and I'll pick you up in about an hour?"

"Okay."

"Oh Deb?"

"Yes?"

"Thanks for taking care of the cat."

Calico's mewing, before a steady drone in the background of the phone call, had turned into wailing. Brent scooped out a generous gourmet feast for her and she quickly changed from wailing back to purring.

***

Magic hour was beginning to set in as Brent and Debbie left for the Santa Barbara Biltmore.

By the time they arrived, the sun was perched above the horizon for another breathtaking Santa Barbara sunset. After the valet fetched the car, they walked across the street to the beach and stood there for a moment to enjoy it. The sky bathed the ocean with an explosion of red, orange and yellow as it descended through the clouds, kissing the horizon. When their eyes met, Brent stroked Debbie's hair and moved in for the kiss.

"Now, that's a homecoming to remember," she said.

It didn't take long, however, for the small talk to turn to business. Debbie was too curious to let it pass. She needed an update. Brent gave her a summary of the bizarre and curtailed interview in the house of horrors that was Camp 7, as well as his own strange treatment at the hands of the Border Patrol upon his arrival in Miami.

"So what's next?" she asked, batting her eyelashes over her baby blues. She may be blonde, but she was no dummy. In fact, she was quite the opposite. As a CPA in the audit department of Ernst & Young, she found talking about Brent's work more interesting than thinking about her own.

"I'll file a habeas corpus petition, and try to get him out of that shit hole. Maybe we can determine what charge he's being held on and get him a hearing."

"They haven't charged him with anything?"

"Not yet. They have a confession with him admitting he came to Iraq to help his brother launder money for al Qaeda."

"That's a serious accusation."

"Apparently, after 20 minutes of waterboarding, not only will you admit allegiance to Osama bin Laden, you'll gladly die just to have relief."

"So the confession was coerced."

"Ya think?"

Brent thought about Ahmed and how free he was in comparison to him. How he had always taken this freedom for granted: The freedom to follow the rules if he found them to be tolerable, and to break them if he found them to be too onerous. Ahmed was only free in his dreams, if that.

CHAPTER FOURTEEN

Brent wasn't sure if he was dreaming or his lips were being rubbed with sandpaper. He felt a heaviness on his chest and a tickling on his face. Upon opening his eyes, he discovered that it was Calico, treating him to some early morning affection as a prelude to her breakfast. As he rolled out of bed, the cat flew off and charged for the kitchen.

Even though it was Saturday, there was no time for leisure. Every minute that Ahmed spent in tortuous confinement was a minute too long. Brent got ready for a long Saturday at the office.

***

The writ of habeas corpus, which literally means, "produce the body," derives from 14th century English law, and is traditionally used to free a person who is wrongfully detained without just cause. It was the only guarantee of a right written into the Constitution itself: The others came in amendments. The ten first amendments were called the "Bill of Rights."

If a petition for habeas corpus is successful, a writ is issued by the court commanding that the prisoner be brought before the court for a hearing to determine whether the custodian has authority to detain the prisoner. If no legal authority is found, the prisoner must be released.

If Ahmed had been held in any prison in the States, obtaining his release would be a relatively simple task, but he was a suspected enemy combatant. Courts had already upheld detentions at Guantanamo under the Authorization for Use of Military Force passed by Congress three days after the September 11th attacks. Given that his "confession" tied him to al Qaeda, the Government would argue that they had the power to hold him indefinitely, or until such time as the military conflict no longer existed.

Because of the destruction of the Afghan and Iraqi infrastructure, the enormous problem of policing, the incredible expense of rebuilding, and the $700 billion U.S. defense budget, it was foreseeable that the "military conflict" there could go on for decades, to the delight of military contractors like Halliburton, Lockheed and General Dynamics. War is good for business.

Robert Kennedy said, "Each time a man stands up for an ideal, or acts to improve the lot of others, or strikes out against injustice, he sends forth a tiny ripple of hope, and crossing each other from a million different centers of energy and daring those ripples to build a current which can sweep down the mightiest walls of oppression and resistance." Brent began work on his own tiny ripple of hope.

Normally a habeas corpus petition had to be filed in the Federal District Court in the district where the prisoner was confined. However, in this case, Brent decided to file in the Central District of California, since Ahmed was incarcerated outside the U.S. but was a United States citizen with a residence in that district.

Ahmed had been denied a cornucopia of basic rights of one normally accused of a crime, including his Sixth Amendment rights to counsel, to a speedy trial, to confront the witnesses against him, to a trial by jury, and the right to be informed of what he was charged with. He had been denied his Fifth Amendment right to a trial by jury, the right to due process, and his coerced confession violated his privilege against self-incrimination. Finally, his treatment at Guantanamo violated his Eighth Amendment right to be free from cruel and unusual punishment.

In any other situation, Brent would have been able to use the notes that he had taken from his interview with Ahmed. But, in Ahmed's case, as was the case with every prisoner in Gitmo, Brent had to turn in all his notes and could not use them until they had been "cleared." Given this handicap, Brent worked from memory.

Brent's request for a visit and examination for Ahmed from the International Red Cross was denied by the military, on the grounds that Ahmed was being held as an "unprivileged enemy combatant," to which the Government considered the Geneva Conventions of 1949 did not apply.

* * *

As Brent worked on the habeas corpus petition, Ahmed paid the price for finally exercising his right to counsel. Armed with Brent's notes, which violated Ahmed's right to counsel and the age-old attorney-client privilege, his captors now had another reason to torture Ahmed: Revenge. It began with Sergeant Brown, of course. Ahmed knew he could count on an early morning visit from him, and that it would be anything but pleasant.

"Your Jew lawyer broke all of our rules, A-hab," Brown said as he entered Ahmed's small cell. "That means no TV, no exercise yard and no toilet privileges for you, Haji."

This was no big deal for Ahmed. He had been forced to soil himself many times during his short captivity. And being shackled to a chair in the TV room was not really his idea of entertainment, just as the 15 minutes per week of exercise he was allowed was not really exercise.

"Since that idiot Jew chickened out, you've been appointed a new lawyer by the Government," added Brown with a smile, "He'll be seeing you soon, so try not to shit yourself."

***

The new lawyer for Ahmed was a young, clean-cut man with a generic American accent. Whereas Ahmed had felt a natural trust for

Brent, he did not feel the same about this new lawyer, Steven Jackson.

"Will you be filing a writ of habeas corpus for me?" Ahmed asked Jackson.

"Well, let's talk about that. We have a hearing coming up before the Combatant Status Review Tribunal. You'll be given an opportunity to show why you shouldn't be designated an enemy combatant. Why do you think a writ of habeas corpus would apply in your case?"

This lawyer must be kidding. "What firm are you with?" asked Ahmed.

"I've been appointed by the Government. Mr. Khury, and I'm asking the questions here. We don't have much time to prepare."

"I'd like to see Mr. Marks."

"Didn't Sergeant Brown tell you he declined representation?"

"Yes, but I prefer to hear that from him. Until I do, I won't be saying anything."

"Suit yourself," said Jackson, with a disappointed frown on his face.

***

After his visit with his new "lawyer," Ahmed was shackled to a chair in a small room and bombarded with strobe lights and loud rock music for hours. It was the equivalent of standing in the first row of the mosh pit at a Black Sabbath concert without earplugs. During this free concert, since he was deprived of his bathroom privileges, Ahmed was forced to pee himself. As the incessant noise droned on, he tried to escape to a peaceful place within his own mind.

Suddenly, after about nine hours, the music and lights stopped. Ahmed's ears were ringing and he continued to see the flashing lights long after they had been turned off. Brown entered the room, grinning with anticipation.

"Listen up A-hab," he declared. "You're going to tell me everything that happened with your Jew lawyer. Tell me everything you talked about, and don't leave anything out."

"I have an attorney-client privilege," Ahmed responded.

"You ain't got no privileges here, Haji."

"Why don't you just listen to the tape?" Ahmed asked.

"Tape?"

"The tape you made from the microphones in the interrogation room."

"You've got an active imagination. I take that you are refusing to cooperate?"

"No, I will tell you anything you want me to."

Ahmed's mind was filled with doubt. *Had Brent Marks really quit? Would he ever see his wife again?* Like a recovering addict, Ahmed vowed to live through the rest of this day without giving up. That would be a battle he would win over his oppressors.

CHAPTER FIFTEEN

Although there was no time, Brent had made a grievance to the U.S. Border Patrol and a civil rights complaint to the Department of Homeland Security on his own detention before his second trip to Cuba. He didn't want to play any more games upon his return to the States. The purpose of this trip was simply to obtain Ahmed's signature on the habeas corpus petition.

John Adams said, "It is more important that innocence be protected than it is that guilt be punished, for guilt and crimes are so frequent in this world that they cannot all be punished." The State gets so carried away with the punishment of evildoers that everyone suffers. As a lawyer, Brent had the unwelcome task of representing criminals throughout his career. When asked why he worked for such "scumbags" his answer was simple. *I'm protecting us all from ourselves.* Out of the 2 million people convicted of crimes every year in the United States, 10,000 of them are innocent, and those are just the statistics that are verifiable.

People are outraged at judges who are seen as "lenient," and they are willing to give up their own rights in exchange for security from the Government. But the only real way to give security to the people is to protect the rights of the innocent.

* * *

When Brent arrived to Camp 7, the X-ray screener confiscated his habeas corpus petition.

"I need that, it's why I came," he told the young soldier.

"It has to go through secondary screening."

"Corporal Reeding, can you please call Sergeant Brown for me. These documents are attorney-client privileged."

"I'll be right back."

The argument with Brown was not one that Brent could possibly win. It ended up with

Brown passing the buck to his commanding officer, Colonel Masters.

***

Colonel Robert Masters was a career soldier, who had earned his birds from the bottom up. His goal was to do the rest of his 20 years, then retire and start working on building a second retirement in another federal job. He had no intention of letting a bleeding heart liberal civilian attorney ruin any of his plans.

"I understand you object to our screening process," said Masters.

"I don't object to your screening process," said Brent. "I object to you looking at communications between myself and my client. And I'm sure your superiors won't take it too kindly if I named you in a lawsuit accusing you of denying my client his right to counsel."

Masters rang his clerk to send in Sergeant Brown, who came in immediately, saluting.

"At ease. Sergeant, give this man his papers."

"Yes, sir."

Brown handed Brent the papers, and Masters dismissed the Sergeant.

"Colonel, there's one more thing."

"What is it?"

"My client's wife would like to visit him."

"No visits are allowed at Camp 7."

"Should I include that in my petition?"

"I'm sorry, sir, that is an item we cannot be flexible on."

Not that they were flexible on anything, thought Brent. Catherine would simply have to wait for the habeas corpus. This news would not sit well with Ahmed.

Before Brent left, Masters asked, "Will you be representing the detainee at his CRST hearing tomorrow?"

"Nobody told me anything about a hearing."

"So you won't be representing him?"

"Of course I will."

***

"I thought you quit," was the first thing that Ahmed said to Brent.

"Is that what they told you?"

"Yes, another attorney came to talk to me. He said he was appointed by the Government."

"He was probably sent to interrogate you. That's one of their interrogation tricks."

"And I thought I knew them all by now."

Ahmed brought Brent up to date on his latest treatment, including a hunger strike among prisoners to protest prison conditions.

"That's a dangerous move," said Brent.

"Every day in here is dangerous."

"Ahmed, please just let me take care of this and get you out of here."

"And when can Catherine come to visit me?"

"Unfortunately, that's not going to happen as long as you're here."

"What if I'm here forever?"

That was a legitimate question, since many of the inmates at Gitmo had been there for years; most without even being charged with anything.

"Just trust me, Ahmed," Brent said, sliding the habeas petition over to him and handing him a pen.

"Oh, I trust you. I just don't trust them. This is their game." Ahmed looked over the petition and signed the back page.

He was right, and the pursuit of justice was also a game, where one man or woman employed by the Government, or sometimes twelve men and women, decided the fate of another. Whether or not that decision was just depended on your point of view. The winner usually thought it was a just result: The loser bore the consequences.

CHAPTER SIXTEEN

The Combatant Status Review Tribunals, or CRSTs, were military tribunals designed to replace the military commissions that President Bush and his cabinet envisioned and created to try, convict and execute their prisoners outside of the United States court system. After the original tribunals were abolished by the Supreme Court in 2006, only to be resurrected by the Military Commissions Act, which abolished the right of habeas corpus: that was also shot down by the Supreme Court in 2008, so the CRSTs were reformed to comply with the Third Geneva Convention. They were not much of an improvement.

Brent didn't have much time at all to prepare for this Kangaroo Court, but he had read some transcripts of proceedings on the

Department of Defense website, so he knew what to expect. The detainee had no rights whatsoever, and it was mainly a show for the military to go through the "evidence," which was presumed to be accurate, that the Government had to determine that the detainee was an enemy combatant. The CRST was supposed to be an independent and neutral body. Most of the proceedings took place in secret.

**

The courtroom for the CRST was a trailer. Brent was provided transport to it as Ahmed's personal representative, and Ahmed was seated in a white chair, with his hands and feet shackled to a bolt in the floor in front of a table draped with a cloth, on which there were placed three microphones in front of three judges chairs, behind which was a mirror on the wall and above that a tiny American flag. A small table held another microphone and recording apparatus for a recorder and a reporter, both of whom were seated when Brent entered the room.

After Brent was seated, three very important looking officers in full uniform took their seats at the draped table. The one in the middle, who had a higher chair, the most important one, spoke.

"Please remain seated and come to order. Please proceed, Recorder."

The Recorder spoke in a nasal monotone, "This tribunal is being conducted at 1009 local time June 5, 2008 on board United States Naval Base Guantanamo Bay, Cuba. The following personnel are present:

"Captain Ulysses Fenmore, United States Navy, President.

"Lieutenant Colonel Joshua Pappie, United States Marine Corps, Member.

"Lieutenant Colonel Daniel Revere, United States Air Force.

"Sergeant Franklin Smith, United States Marine Corps.

"Reporter Lieutenant Jackson Devlin, United States Navy, Recorder.

"Captain Thomas Grant is the Judge Advocate Member of the tribunal.

"All rise," said the Recorder, and the Kangaroo Court went through its pomp and circumstance, swearing in the reporter, the recorder, and then rising again to swear in the members of the tribunal.

"Mr. Brent Marks, I understand that you will be acting as personal representative of the detainee, is that correct?" asked Captain Fenmore.

"Yes, Captain."

"Mr. Marks, I am the president of the tribunal. You will address me as Mr. President."

"Yes, Mr. President."

"The Recorder will swear in the personal representative."

"Do you swear or affirm that you will faithfully perform the duties or personal representative in this tribunal, so help you God?"

"I do," said Brent.

"Please be seated," said Captain Fenmore. "Mr. Marks, are you advising the tribunal that the detainee has elected not to participate in this tribunal proceeding?"

"No, Mr. President. The very fact that he is seated here with his hands and feet bolted to your floor evidences his participation. The detainee also has a name, sir. It is Ahmed Khury, and he has decided to invoke his Fifth Amendment right to remain silent during these proceedings.'

"Mr. Marks, we granted an exception to allow you to act as personal representative, rather than an officer. I'm sure you were briefed as to the rules of this tribunal, were you not?"

"Yes, I was, Mr. President."

"Then you should know, sir, that the Fifth Amendment does not apply in these proceedings. However, the detainee will not be forced to make any testimony."

"I am aware that you believe that the Constitution itself does not apply to these proceedings or to the way you treat the prisoners."

"Recorder, please provide the tribunal with the unclassified evidence," said the Captain.

The Recorder held out a report in his hand. "I am handing the tribunal what has been previously marked as Exhibit R-1, the unclassified summary that relates to the Detainee's status as an enemy combatant. A copy of this exhibit was provided to the personal representative in advance of this hearing for presentation to the Detainee."

The report was a "fill in the blanks" form surveillance report that had been completed by military intelligence, giving a paint by numbers picture of Ahmed as a sleeper cell reuniting with his jihadist brothers.

"Objection, hearsay," said Brent.

"Mr. Marks, the rules of evidence don't apply to this proceeding."

"It seems that no rules apply, Mr. President. Why don't you just make your findings right now? We all know what they are going to be."

"Mr. Marks, you will respect our procedures. The Recorder will read the unclassified summary of evidence for the record."

The Recorder read through a report, recounting surveillance on Ahmed's brother, Sabeen, his suspecting money laundering activities, alleged ties to al Qaeda, and their capture in Iraq. It was mainly a "guilt by association" report, detailing Sabeen's friends, who were suspected al-Qaeda sleeper cells.

Next, Ahmed's transcribed "confession," extracted from his waterboarding session, was introduced.

"Objection, Mr. President. This document cannot possibly be used as evidence. It violates Mr. Khury's Sixth Amendment right to counsel, his Fifth Amendment privilege against self-incrimination, his Eighth Amendment right to be free from cruel and unusual punishment, and over 50 years of case law against the admission of coerced confessions."

"Once again, Mr. Marks, these principles do not apply to this tribunal."

"If these principles don't apply, Mr. President, then just what exactly are you fighting for in Afghanistan, and Iraq? Why have so many of our American boys died there? Defending what? The right to obliterate the Constitution and everything it stands for? The right to treat our fellow man as if he is some kind of an insect instead of a human being? Is that what we have come to? If that is what you think America stands for, Captain, I don't know how you can say that you are proud to be an American."

The Captain stood up in a rage. "How dare you impugn the integrity of this tribunal? My patriotism is not in question here. Mr. Marks, I will hold you in contempt if there are any further comments like those."

"Understood Mr. President, your patriotism is not in issue. I've had my say."

The Recorder then read into the record Ahmed's coerced confession.

"Does the Detainee wish to present any evidence?"

"No, Mr. President."

"Recorder, do you have any further unclassified evidence?"

"No sir, Mr. President, that concludes the presentation of the unclassified evidence, but I respectfully request a closed tribunal session at an appropriate time to present classified evidence."

"Recorder, your request for a closed session is granted and it will be taken in due course. We will now pause briefly for the tribunal members to read the classified evidence."

The three military chiefs looked as important as three toads sitting on the biggest lily pads in the pond, as they read through the secret evidence that neither Brent nor Ahmed had the right to see.

"We will now allow for the calling of witnesses. All witnesses called before this tribunal may be questioned by the Detainee, if present, the personal representative, the Recorder, and the tribunal members. Does the Recorder have any witnesses to present?"

"No, sir."

"On the Detainee election form provided to the tribunal earlier, I note the Detainee has not requested any witnesses to be present. Does any member of the tribunal have any questions for the personal representative or the Recorder at this time?"

"No, sir."

"No, sir."

"All unclassified evidence having been presented to the tribunal, this concludes the open tribunal session. The Detainee, Ahmed Khury shall be notified of the tribunal decision upon completion of the review of these proceedings by the Combatant Status Review Tribunal Convening Authority in Washington, D.C. If the tribunal determines that the Detainee should not be classified as an enemy combatant, he will be released to his home country as soon as arrangements can be made."

Fat chance of that happening, Brent thought.

"The Administrative Review Board will make an assessment of whether there is continued reason to believe that the Detainee poses a threat to the United States or its coalition partners in the ongoing armed conflict against terrorist organizations such as al Qaeda and its affiliates and supporters or whether there are other factors bearing upon the continued need for detention."

With the cold mechanical canned read with the, "insert-the-blanks for the name," the mock court proceedings had come to an end.

CHAPTER SEVENTEEN

Laura Ingalls Wilder said, "Home is the nicest place there is." As Brent was flying home from Cuba, he was looking forward to being in that special place. But, unbeknownst to him, a different part of the game was being played out in Santa Barbara. Agents of the FBI Special Terrorist Task Force paid a surprise visit to Catherine Khurys' home while she was at work.

The Fourth Amendment to the United States Constitution, intact for over 200 years, guaranteed that the right of the people to be secure in their persons, houses, papers and effects, against unreasonable searches and seizures, shall not be violated, and no warrants shall issue, but upon probable cause, supported by oath of affirmation, and particularly describing the place to be searched, and the persons or things to be seized. After September

11th, 2001, those were just words on an old piece of paper, no longer a restriction of the Government's overreaching power to shake down its subjects.

Without a warrant, and in the name of national security, four Special Agents with weapons drawn entered the Foothill Road home and personal sanctuary of suspected terrorist Ahmed Khury, his wife Catherine, and their family, secretly, without knocking and announcing their presence, as authorized by the Patriot Act. The only one they had to convince to open the door was the locksmith.

The agents shuffled by the two pairs of large shoes and two pairs of small shoes neatly arranged in the corridor and trampled the soft plush carpet of the Khury's cozy living room, once reserved for shoeless feet. There, they opened every drawer and cabinet and carefully looked through all the contents, searching for anything that might be incriminating.

Inviting himself for a stroll through the Khury's memories, one agent trespassed through the Khury's family albums: their wedding, the birth of their first child, Karen, her first steps, their son Cameron, his first tentative ride on a bicycle. The agent helped himself to randomly selected pictures of Ahmed, Catherine and their two children, and placed them into a plastic bag.

He continued to pore over every photo album, and removed pictures of Ahmed and "other Arabs."

As another agent looked through each CD and DVD in the storage space in their television cabinet, the third agent removed pillows from the couches and looked in the crevices for more "evidence" that may uncover terrorist activity. The fourth busied himself with fixing listening devices to the lamps in the room.

Moving into the kitchen, the agents examined every drawer and cabinet, the interior of the refrigerator and even the oven. But their jackpot came in the den, which contained a desk and two computers. Two agents scooped up the laptop and PC, and took them to the van waiting outside.

The computers would be examined for any evidence of terrorist activity or money laundering. Every social network account of Ahmed and his wife would be monitored. Their bank accounts, securities accounts, and even their Facebook and email accounts would never be private again. No need to worry about changing passwords any more.

Each of the two guest bedrooms was thoroughly searched. Three agents breached the sanctity of Ahmed and Catherine's master bedroom, tugged on the bedspread that only their children had done before, and put their unwashed hands between the sheets where they had once made love.

Their "his and hers" closets were carefully examined. Every article of clothing had strange hands put on it, including the intimates in Catherine's underwear drawer.

"Found a cell phone," happily declared one agent, as he threw it into an evidence bag.

After the examination of the garage, the violation of the Khurys' home was complete. The agents slipped away as quietly as they had come, without a hint of their presence left behind, except for the missing items of personal property.

CHAPTER EIGHTEEN

Corporal Reeding strapped Ahmed's shackled arms and legs into the black and grey steel and vinyl restraint chair, and immobilized his head with a large black leather band, which he tightened like a belt buckle. Next to the chair, on a small steel tray covered with plastic and paper were an assortment of tubes, gauze and plastic bags, and a bottle of "Ensure" protein shake.

"What are you going to do to me?" asked Ahmed, in terror, as he wondered what kind of torture was in store for him this time, "I told you everything I know. I answered all of your questions," he added.

"This isn't an interrogation. You're going to be fed because you refused your meal."

"I wasn't hungry. What's going on Corporal Reeding?"

"You said you wanted to die."

"Of course I said that when I was being tortured! You would say it too!"

Reeding stepped back and a male Navy nurse stood in his place. Now, Reeding's job was just to observe. He had been put on force-feeding detail going on only three days, and the entire process disgusted him.

"Who are you? What are you going to do to me?" Ahmed asked the nurse.

"I am going to perform an enteral feeding procedure. We will pass a naso-enteral feeding tube through your nose to your stomach to give you the nutrition you need to survive."

"This really isn't necessary," said Ahmed. "I was just not hungry."

"I have my orders," said the nurse. "Would you prefer lidocaine` or should I lubricate the feeding tube with some olive oil?" he asked.

"I don't know."

The nurse opened a small package, lubricated the end of the feeding tube with its contents, and then shoved the tube into Ahmed's left nostril. Ahmed cried out in pain and choked on the tube as the nurse continued to push it through his nose, down his throat and into his stomach. Ahmed watched in horror as the tube was pushed further and further down his nose. He tried to move away from the intruding tube to expel it from his body, but he could not turn his head. He felt the tube scratching against his throat, and coughed uncontrollably until the tube came out of his nose.

The nurse dabbed Ahmed's bloody left nostril with gauze and again lubricated the tube with lidocaine.

"No, no, please don't! I will eat! I will eat!"

This time he inserted the tube into Ahmed's right nostril. Ahmed's hands and feet pushed instinctively against the restraints as he felt the tube penetrating his nose, throat and finally his stomach, which gave him the urge to vomit. Ahmed choked, tried to breathe, and, in his panic, began to hyperventilate. There was a fire in his chest.

"You must calm down," said the nurse. "We're not going to hurt you."

"You're hurting me now," Ahmed gasped. "I can't, I can't breathe."

"Calm down and breathe normally."

Ahmed tried to calm himself down. He went to the place where he always went when they tortured him. The place where he and Catherine, Cameron and Karen were free to laugh and play together. He dreamed of them holding hands, strolling the deserted beach below the cliffs of Shoreline Park. They used to go there and sit for hours, watching dolphins swim by and listening to the sea lions bark. As he dreamed, he began to breathe in and out of his mouth and his respiration calmed. He imagined being in the park with the kids, and pushing them in their swings as they called out, "Higher! Higher!"

Ahmed choked as the liquid passed through the tube and into his stomach. He sat there, immobilized, for about 20 minutes for the feeding, but for Ahmed it seemed an eternity. When the nurse finally pulled the tube out, the experience of removal was almost as bad as the insertion, giving Ahmed the urge to vomit. The nurse stuffed Ahmed's bloody right nostril with gauze. As Ahmed choked and sputtered, the nurse put a mask over his face, and he threw up in the mask, covering his face with his own vomit.

***

Brent placed a luscious bite of lobster thermidor in his mouth, savoring the creamy mixture. Debbie the "blonde bombshell" looked on affectionately.

"This beats the airline food I've been on lately."

"I should say. Do you have to go back to that place?"

"Only if the judge holds an evidentiary hearing. I'd want to go and depose witnesses to preserve their testimony."

"So what's the next step?"

"We file the habeas petition, the Government files an opposition, and we try to get him tried in District Court or released."

Debbie's home cooking was great, but the company was even better. As the candles dwindled, they drained the bottle of Pinot Grigio. Brent's thoughts drifted to Ahmed. It's true that life is a balance between hardship and joy. Everybody suffers. But in Ahmed's case the balance was decidedly tipped toward suffering, and the joy was only in his memories.

CHAPTER NINETEEN

Thomas Jefferson said in his inaugural address that "habeas corpus secures every man here, alien or citizen, against everything which is not law, whatever shape it may assume."

Finally, one month after the filing of his petition, and after two months in custody, Ahmed would have his day in court. The only difference is that he would not be there.

Built in 1940, the U.S. Courthouse in Los Angeles was a granite and terra cotta masterpiece of art deco architecture. Judge Henley's courtroom on Spring Street was paneled in dark wood, with strips of travertine marble in between the panels and high ceilings. Two counsel tables on the left and right were joined at the middle by a speaking podium. There was a vast no man's land between the counsel tables and the clerk's table, which was situated just below the judge's lofty bench. The jury box was on the right, a table for the judge's clerks on the left, and the seating gallery had church-style wooden pews.

U.S. District Court Judge Matthew Henley was a former U.S. Attorney who had a stellar prosecutorial record. He was known as a judge who was tough on crime. Federal judges are appointed, not elected, so, once in their seats, they have no reason to bend to popular opinion. Henley was no exception. He was tough on crime because he thought that judges should be tough on crime.

Brent was hoping that, with his experience, Judge Henley would be so offended by the lack of due process that had been afforded a fellow citizen, no matter of what crime he had been accused, that he would not let his feelings about crime deter him from doing what was right. Brent was encouraged that the judge did not decide the petition without a hearing. This probably meant that he wanted to hear argument. So far, however, even on the day before the hearing, there was no indication that he had made any tentative ruling on the petition.

Upon Brent's arrival to the courtroom, he first noticed his opponent, Stephen Gray, of the U.S. Attorney's office, frustratingly going over his notes, looking defeated. That was a good sign. Brent found the judge's tentative ruling on the counsel table, checked in with the clerk, then started to read the tentative. Judges seldom change their minds after issuing a tentative ruling but Judge Henley would give the lawyers their say in trying to convince him to change his mind.

Brent sat in the wooden pew in a half-filled courtroom, reading the tentative. It was a landslide victory. Henley ruled that Ahmed's confession was coerced, in violation of his Fifth Amendment privilege against self-incrimination and his Sixth Amendment right to counsel, since his pleas for speaking to his lawyer had been ignored, as well as a denial of his right to habeas corpus under the Habeas Corpus Suspension Clause of the Constitution. As such, the confession could not be used to determine that he was an enemy combatant that the military could hold without charge.

He noted that "the Government's position that the Constitution had no effect at Guantanamo Bay caused great separation-of-powers concerns, and that, the president was not allowed to simply 'turn the Constitution off' simply because Guantanamo, which had been under U.S. control for over 100 years, was in a foreign country. This ruling, if allowed to stand, would direct the issuance of a writ of habeas corpus to Guantanamo Bay prison, releasing Ahmed to the U.S. Marshal, where he would be held in California, pending the Government charging him within the next 72 hours. If they failed to charge him with any crime, he would be released.

Brent went over his speaking notes while trying to ignore the proceedings that were going on with other cases on the judge's calendar. No matter how many times he had done this for over 18 years, the adrenalin always flowed at top capacity in anticipation of speaking. Sometimes the judge let you speak, sometimes it turned into a Q&A, and sometimes it amounted to an intellectual game of chess between two jurists: a sort of intelligence-pissing contest with the deck stacked in favor of the court.

The law is logical and is based on common sense. The trick was to argue the law in favor of your particular point of view without sounding biased. It was kind of like a magic trick: the best illusionist being the one who can best manipulate the logic to his or her advantage, all the while giving the illusion of impartiality.

Judge Henley's clerk called the case, and Brent stepped up to the podium, his heart pounding with the knowledge that, whatever he said or did not say may make a difference in whether Ahmed was set free or spent the rest of his life in detention. Stephen Gray followed Brent and weighed in for the match, equally burdened with the onerous responsibility of upholding the war on terror.

"Mr. Gray, the tentative is against the Government, so I would like to hear from you first," said Judge Henley. "I know I shouldn't have to say this, but I've read the petition and the opposition, and what I really want to hear is what is not in the moving or opposing papers."

"Yes, Your Honor. I don't have to remind the court that, on September 11, 2001, the United States of America was viciously attacked by al Qaeda, whose attack on New York City killed over three thousand innocent people. The Authorization for Military Force that was issued in response to this attack is a Congressional Act which gives the president the power to detain any individual who is part of forces associated with the Taliban or al Qaeda in order to defeat this terrorist threat to our nation.

"The Government has shown that it is more likely than not that Mr. Khury has materially supported al Qaeda's money laundering operation, which gives it the right to detain Mr. Khury. In his order, President Bush has determined that Mr. Khury is an enemy combatant, engaged in conduct preparing for international terrorism aimed at the United States, and represents a present and continuing danger to national security. This power gives the president the right to hold Mr. Khury until such time as hostilities in Iraq have ceased."

"Mr. Gray," said the judge, interrupting. "You stated that the Authorization for Use of Military Force is a Congressional Act. If so, the Non-Detention Act would not apply in this case. I'm not convinced that the Authorization for Use of Military Force is a Congressional Act. Convince me."

"Your honor, the United States Supreme Court, in *Hamdi v. Rumsfeld,* held that the Authorization to Use Military Force was, indeed, a Congressional Act, and that the detention of an individual designated as an enemy combatant did not violate the Anti-Detention Act."

"Please proceed Mr. Gray."

"Your Honor, the Defense Department has established Combatant Status Review Tribunals to determine whether individuals detained at Guantanamo are enemy combatants. That determination was made in Mr. Khury's case."

"But, Mr. Gray, the Tribunals are established by the military. Therefore, they exist under the President's Article I authority. They are not Article III courts."

"I understand that, Your Honor, but, the Detainee Treatment Act of 2005 gives the D.C.

District Court exclusive jurisdiction to review Tribunal decisions. With all due respect, Your Honor, this Court does not have jurisdiction.

"Even if this Court did have jurisdiction, Your Honor, the decisions of the D.C. Circuit Court of Appeals which are cited in my briefs, and which leave individual cases to be resolved according to their circumstances, clearly support the Government's contention that the Authorization for Military Force authorizes the detention of not only those who are part of al-Qaeda and the Taliban, but those who purposefully and materially support them.

"This is what the Government has alleged against Mr. Khury. Al Qaeda, the Taliban, and associated forces still pose a grave threat to national security, and the Authorization for Military Force still empowers the president to address the continuing threat posed by these groups."

CHAPTER TWENTY

Ahmed's mind drifted to the federal courtroom in California and he imagined what was going on there, as the guard opened the food port, or "splash box" in his small cell, slid in a tray, and then locked the port. Today was the most important day of his life, and the last thing he could think about was food. On top of that, it had been only one day since he had been released from the force-feeding program. His nostrils were sore, his throat bruised and scratched, and his stomach was churning with acid. His chest was burning, he was hot, and sweating profusely. Nevertheless, he scooped up as much as the gruel as he could, swallowing it as fast as he could, which was probably a mistake, because, after he did, he felt the instant urge to throw up.

Ahmed's two weeks on the force-feeding program had turned him into a virtual skeleton. The last thing he had expected that day was a visit from Sergeant Brown, who entered the cell just as Ahmed was throwing up in the toilet.

"Wassa matter A-hab? Not happy to see me?"

"Of course, Sergeant Brown, I'm always happy to see you," said Ahmed, wiping the vomit off his lips with the back of his hand.

"You know, you can't avoid eating by pretending you're bulimic."

"Sergeant Brown, I swear, I just got sick. I have no reason to refuse food."

"You think your fancy lawyer's gonna get you outta here A-hab? You ain't never leavin' our country club."

"Whatever you say, Sergeant Brown."

"And don't worry about your lunch, we have a special menu, just for you."

"No Sergeant Brown, please! I'll eat another tray of regular food, please, sir!"

Brown grinned, turned and left, slamming the solid steel door behind him. Dostoyevsky said, "People sometimes speak about the bestial cruelty of man, but that is terribly unjust and offensive to beasts, no animal could ever be so cruel as a man, so artfully, so artistically cruel."

***

Judge Henley turned the podium over to Brent, but not until he had thrown his planned speech off with a poignant question. "Mr. Marks, Mr. Gray raises a very important issue. Why do you think this Court has jurisdiction in this case? Why should this petition not be heard by the D.C. Circuit Court in accordance with the Detainee Treatment Act of 2005, as the Government asserts?"

"Your Honor, the Detainee Treatment Act, although relevant to the horrendous torture that Mr. Khury has endured during his military detention, has provisions that limits relief to aliens detained at Guantanamo. The Supreme Court has just held in *Boumedine vs. Bush* that detainees need not seek review of their Tribunal decisions in the D.C. Circuit as a prerequisite to proceeding with a habeas action in District Court. Mr. Khury is a United States citizen, not an alien, and, as such, he has an undeniable right to have his case heard by an Article III court, not a military tribunal. Being a resident of Southern California, that is your court, Your Honor."

"Thank you, Mr. Marks, please proceed."

"Thank you, Your Honor. For over two centuries, through times of war and times of peace, the Bill of Rights to the United States Constitution has guaranteed that nobody would be deprived of liberty without due process of law. As the Supreme Court noted in *Boumediene vs. Bush,* "Security subsists infidelity to freedom's first principles. Chief among those is freedom from arbitrary and unlawful restraint and the personal liberty that is secured by the adherence to the separation of powers."

"Yet, for over two months, the Government has held Ahmed Khury in captivity, without alleging that he has taken up arms against the United States; in fact, it has not charged him with anything. The sole reason given for his indefinite detention is the executive's belief that he can seize and detain him indefinitely on the allegation that he is an enemy combatant.

"Even assuming the Government's allegations are true, that Mr. Khury has indeed assisted with a money laundering operation to benefit al Qaeda, albeit based on a coerced confession, which I will discuss later, this allegation, however serious, is not enough to make Mr. Khury an enemy combatant. He has never taken up arms against the United States nor has he assisted any person to do so. Mr.

Khury has never been given the opportunity to dispute his enemy combatant status in an Article III court, and he should be allowed to do so with full criminal process."

"Whether the Detention Act applies or not, the fundamental notion of due process is at the heart of our nation's foundation as a nation of laws. If we cease to follow the law, the United States will also cease to be a nation of laws. Therefore, we can't really entertain a discussion of whether or not Mr. Khury is an enemy combatant without discussing the more important issue of due process.

"The Supreme Court, in *Hamdi v. Rumsfeld,* held that a citizen being accused of being an enemy combatant is entitled to full notice of the factual basis for this determination and a fair opportunity to rebut the Government's case before a neutral decision maker."

"Mr. Marks, wasn't the Supreme Court's ruling in *Hamdi v. Rumsfeld* limited to the case of a U.S. citizen held on American soil?"

"Your Honor, it is true that the Hamdi case concerned a citizen held on U.S. soil, but, in the case of U.S. citizens, whether they are held by the military on U.S. soil or by the military in a foreign country, they are still entitled to the basic due process rights of notice of what they are

119

being held for and an opportunity to be heard to challenge that charge. President Bush has adopted the belief, however ill-advised that may be, that the executive can put anyone he determines is an enemy combatant in military detention, without ever giving them a trial. This is not consistent with due process."

"But, Mr. Marks, the USA Patriot Act authorizes detention of a suspected terrorist without charge, does it not?"

"Yes, Your Honor, but not indefinite detention. That's the difference here. My client has been detained indefinitely without due process. There have been no formal charges levied against him, nor has he had the right to be heard in a court of law regarding the sufficiency of those charges. He should be charged, and given the opportunity to face those charges, or he should be released."

***

As the arguments continued in federal court, Corporal Reeding and his force-feeding team came to collect Ahmed from his cell.

"Please, Corporal Reeding, I was just sick. I will eat, I really will!"

"Sorry Ahmed, we have our orders."

"No! No!"

The members of the detail shackled Ahmed's ankles and hands, hooded him, and dragged him out of his cell for the long walk to the force-feeding area. Ahmed's nasal passages and throat, already swollen and scraped from two weeks of force-feeding, were about to undergo another full frontal assault.

Corporal Reeding strapped Ahmed into the force-feeding chair, and the nurse lubricated the tip of the feeding tube with olive oil, as usual, and then shoved the tube into an unwilling Ahmed.

The nurse had difficulty with the tube, and Ahmed coughed it up twice. Finally, the nurse forced the tube down Ahmed's right nostril, which caused another bout of coughing. His chest was on fire, and he felt that the tube was not reaching his stomach.

"It's not in right! I feel like the tube is at the bottom of my throat!" Ahmed pleaded with the nurse, who replied, "It's just fine, don't worry," and proceeded to drip in the solution.

Ahmed choked. He felt like he was drowning. He tried to speak, but he couldn't. He felt as if he would pass out, and finally coughed up a pink solution of Ensure mixed with blood.

"Stop the procedure!" said Reeding. The nurse looked up in shock, and removed the feeding tube from a sputtering Ahmed, whose body then went limp.

***

At the end of the arguments, Brent was not sure if Judge Henley had been convinced to stick with his tentative or not. He, Ahmed and Catherine would have to wait for the judge to reflect on the arguments and render his written decision.

***

Corporal Reinhart, a 22-year-old from Macon, Georgia, looked into the portal of Ahmed's cell on a routine check and saw Ahmed hanging naked from the wire mesh ceiling by his jumpsuit. The Corporal sounded the alarm, and Sergeant Brown came running.

"What is it Corporal?"

"It looks like the Haji hanged himself, sir."

Brown unlocked the steel door and cut Ahmed down while Corporal Reinhart held his limp body. Ahmed's face was pale.

"Go get the doctor!" yelled Brown, as he checked Ahmed's pulse.

CHAPTER TWENTY-ONE

The very evening of the same day in court, Judge Henley issued a writ of habeas corpus to "produce the body" of Ahmed Khury. The sorry detail was that the body of Ahmed Khury was no longer alive. The Naval Criminal Investigative Service (NCIS) had already issued a report calling it a probable suicide and an autopsy had already been performed under NCIS's orders.

Brent was the first to be informed of his client's demise. The news came in an early morning phone call from Stephen Gray.

"Brent, it's Stephen Gray."

"Stephen, did you see the ruling?"

"Yes, I did, but that's not why I called."

"Why then?"

"Brent, I don't know how to tell you this, so I'll just say it. Your client was found dead this morning in his cell."

"Found dead? What does it mean, found dead?"

"NCIS is calling it an apparent suicide."

"Suicide…"

"Yes, he hanged himself in his cell."

"Stephen, listen to me carefully, I do not want anyone to touch the body."

"Too late, they've already done an autopsy."

"Well, that's very convenient. This is a lot to take in at one time, you know. I need that autopsy report, and I need the body."

"We'll arrange for the body to be transported back to California, but I'm afraid the autopsy report is classified."

"Then get it de-classified, Stephen. This is too hard to believe. My client commits suicide on the eve of his writ of habeas corpus? I don't buy it."

"I'll see what I can do to get you the report."

"Please do that. Has anyone told his wife?"

"No."

"Good, let me do it, alright? I don't want her to get some drone monotone phone call from someone whom she doesn't know and doesn't give two shits about her or her husband."

"Of course Brent. I'm sorry."

"Not your fault Stephen. It's probably your bosses' fault, but definitely not yours. You were just doing your job."

"I'm just serving my country, Brent."

"I know. Me too. I just can't believe what it's come to."

***

The birds chirped happily in the charming Santa Barbara neighborhood that held the home of Ahmed and Catherine Khury and their two children. Although Southern California is not known for the changing of seasons, the thick trunked maple trees on E. Haley Street had released a collage assortment of yellows, reds and oranges onto the sidewalk below, signaling the arrival of autumn to the unknowing state and its occupants. Brent knocked on the door, and Catherine opened it, surprised.

"Mr. Marks, hello."

"Hello Catherine."

"Won't you come in, please?"

Catherine ushered Brent in to her home, and he removed his shoes, putting them next to the other pairs of shoes that were in the corridor.

"You don't have to do that, Mr. Marks. But look there, where you put your shoes. I have left Ahmed's shoes there, for when he comes home. Please, sit down. Tell me your news."

Brent sat down and broke the unthinkable news to Catherine in one terribly awkward and uncomfortable sentence.

"Catherine, I'm so sorry to give you this news, but Ahmed has died."

The room around Catherine exploded from the shock, the sorrow, and then the grief of the news she had just heard. Through her tears, she tried to speak.

"Why? Why did this happen? How could this happen?"

"I don't know, Catherine."

"Why did this happen to my beautiful Ahmed? What is their explanation of this?"

"They say he hung himself in his cell."

"That's ridiculous! Ahmed was hoping for the habeas corpus to be granted."

"And it was."

"The Court says he can come home and now he's dead! When can I have my Ahmed back? He has suffered enough. I need to lay him to rest."

"It's being arranged. Catherine, if you allow me, we can punish those responsible for this."

"I can't, I can't right now…"

"I know. We can talk about it later."

Despite the devastation inside the Khury home, the loss of a husband, a lover, a father; despite the fact that the world would never be the same again for them, outside, the birds were still chirping and the leaves still falling. An endless cycle of cruelty had been hidden behind the beautiful façade of nature.

PART II

FIGHTING CITY HALL

CHAPTER TWENTY-TWO

Ahmed's body was flown back to California, where it underwent another assault, this time at the request of his wife. Brent had recommended Dr. Jaime Orozco, a medical examiner for the autopsy, who was a former forensic pathologist for the FBI. The NCIS autopsy was still classified, so Dr. Orozco was called upon to perform an independent pathological examination. Brent met Dr. Orozco in his office to discuss his preliminary findings.

Orozco had more than a few extra pounds to haul around. He reminded Brent a bit of all the characters he had seen in movies and TV shows where the doctors were always munching on a sandwich or something while they were doing autopsies. But he was smart, and Brent thought he would make a good expert witness notwithstanding his personal appearance.

133

"I'm not so sure if we have a suicide here," said Orozco. He cleared his throat as if he was gargling his saliva.

"Why?"

"Were they force-feeding Mr. Khury? I found traces of the liquid nutrient Ensure in his lungs."

"I don't know if they were or not."

"And I found traces of olive oil in his nostrils and lungs as well, so I ran a check on his lung tissues for lipoid pneumonia, and it looks like he had it."

"What does it mean, doctor?"

"It means that I think they were force-feeding Mr. Khury in captivity, and that they used olive oil to lubricate the feeding tube. That is, in my opinion an instance of negligent medical care in reckless disregard of standard medical practices."

"So you don't think it was suicide? You think his death was due to negligence?"

"I do. But not from his lipoid pneumonia, although that probably did weaken his respiration. It appears that they inserted the feeding tube improperly, resulting in his aspirating the feeding fluid."

"And this will be the conclusion in your report?"

"Yes, despite the fact that we don't have the stomach contents from the previous autopsy and the lungs have been dissected, there is still enough evidence to draw this conclusion."

"Thank you doctor. I can't say that his wife will be pleased, because nothing would please her right now, but for her to know it wasn't suicide will come as somewhat a relief."

"I understand. I sure would like to see that Navy autopsy report."

"It's still classified. But I'm working on getting it with a Freedom of Information request."

∗∗∗

As Brent had expected, the news brought a mixed reaction from Catherine. It had been difficult enough to get her to agree to a second autopsy.

"Thank you for everything you've done, Mr. Marks. But I don't know where we are going with this."

"Capturing Ahmed was wrong, Catherine. And even if he did the things he was accused of, he was denied basic rights that they're not allowed to take away from anybody."

"Ahmed didn't do those things. He loved America. He was a fanatic about how great America was."

"I hate to bring this up at this time, Catherine, but I think you have a good case against the Government for wrongful death. It won't ease your sorrow, but it may help a lot of people in the future."

"Mr. Marks, I can't even afford to pay your bill on the habeas corpus. How could I possibly sue the Government?"

"Don't worry about the bill. I'm going to waive the unpaid amount. As for the new case, I would take it on a contingency. If we don't get a settlement or judgment, I don't get paid."

"It just doesn't seem right to ask for money, Mr. Marks. Ahmed was priceless to me. No amount of money can make up for him not being here."

"I know. But it's the only way to make a stand against the horrible things that the Government is doing in the name of fighting terrorism. There's a case out of Oregon that was successful where an American citizen was captured and held as an enemy combatant and his home and personal effects were searched without warrant, just like with you."

"So I would be suing the Government for Ahmed's death, and…"

"And the violation of your civil rights. We would be attacking the entire process set up for capturing and trying suspected terrorists without due process and the Patriot Act."

"What's the Patriot Act?"

"The USA Patriot Act was signed a month after the terrorist attacks of 2001 as part of the "War on Terror." It authorized the indefinite detention of immigrants, the searching of a home or business without the owner's knowledge, as well as telephone, email, library and financial records without a court order."

"Like they did to us."

"Yes. The Patriot Act has practically obliterated the Fourth Amendment to the Constitution. It was supposed to be temporary, but there are so many things that the Government likes about the power that it gives, they keep renewing it."

"I think it's time for this Patriot Act to die, Mr. Marks. My family didn't do anything."

"I'm with you, Catherine. Just leave it to me."

CHAPTER TWENTY-THREE

Brent went to work immediately to prepare a claim against the U.S. Government pursuant to the Federal Tort Claims Act. The Government must give its "consent" to be sued, so the Act required Brent to make a claim to the Government first. After it was denied, Brent would be free to file the lawsuit.

In the meantime, Brent pushed through a Freedom of Information Act request for the release of the report of the military autopsy. He was helped in this regard by the most unlikely of people: Assistant U.S. Attorney Stephen Gray. Stephen had convinced the NCIS to de-classify the report, given the fact that Mrs. Khury had filed a claim against the Government for Ahmed's wrongful death.

When the report arrived, despite the conclusion that the cause of death was suicide by hanging, it held several other findings that Dr. Orozco found to be pertinent, such as traces of olive oil in the nasal passages and trachea, and traces of Ensure in the lungs. Given that the same evidence was cited in both reports, and that only the opinion differed, it would be a battle between experts when the dispute found its way to a courtroom.

***

Brent sent Rick Penn out to track down every serviceman who was Stateside, who had ever served at the Guantanamo prisons. With home leave and most of the young men on two year or less revolving deployments, it wasn't long before he had a string of them to interview.

The army is trained to survive the horror and slaughter of modern day warfare. Part of that training instills an undying loyalty toward their country, and an even higher loyalty toward their fellow soldiers. This dedication is forged into them like steel and it survives the end of their tour, persisting as a life principle. After several interviews, Rick was sure that he was not going to come away from any of them with a bit of useful information.

***

Brent picked Rick up at the airport, anxious to learn of his progress. He spotted Rick when he walked into the baggage claim area at Terminal 7. Rick greeted him with a worn out smile.

"I see who won all the battles," he said to Rick.

"It's like the most organized Old Boys' Club in the world."

"Nobody's talking?"

"Nope. Names, ranks, and serial numbers. That's about it."

"Well, you know what Thomas Edison said."

"What?"

"I have not failed. I've just found 10,000 ways that won't work."

"That's encouraging Brent, thanks."

CHAPTER TWENTY-FOUR

The Jarhead was a favorite military hangout in Beaufort, South Carolina, home to three military bases: Parris Island, the Marine boot camp center, the Marine Corps Air Station and the Naval Hospital. It was a place to hang out, let off some steam, blow your paycheck.

The smell of stale beer that had spilled and soaked into the wood over the years mixed with the perfume steaming from the three sluts hanging out together at the bar. They were looking for a few good men themselves, their ready lips slicked with blood red lipstick, cheeks packed with too much cake-up, and their skinny bodies stuffed into skimpy costumes, carefully designed to flash a little T there and a little A there. The dingy light from the two TV sets above the bar playing ESPN 24/7 reflected the hungry faces of the testosterone overloaded guys on liberty, all on the hunt for a little pink hand to hand combat.

A live band played Chili Peppers to the clacking rhythm with the three pool tables, busy with the sounds of competition and small core gambling. Seated in the small dark alcove were four devildogs with crew cuts, the only serious men in the entire joint, chain-smoking and amassing an impressive collection of butts.

"Man, this is FUBAR," said one of them, a skinny tall guy, as he took a drag off the last morsel of cigarette, then smashed it in the ashtray like he was squashing a bug.

"Yeah Skinny, but what can we do about it?" added another, a dumb looking kid who they called "Rock," because his mouth was always hanging open like a retard.

"Plenty, Maggot. We're Marines. I've got a plan," said a cocky little dude with wild eyes they called 'Balls,' because he had the balls to do just about anything. "It's gonna be a secret mission, so you all have to agree to follow my lead."

"What's the plan?" asked the fourth, a freckled boy who was always nervous, whom they had nicknamed, "Pumpkin Head."

"We all swore to defend the United States against all enemies, foreign and domestic, right?" They all chimed in agreement between gulps of beer.

"I heard talk at Gitmo that there's a domestic enemy right here Stateside cozying up to the fucking Hajis and going after our Brass in the courts."

"That civilian lawyer? The one defending the dead Haji?" asked Rock.

"Pretty smart, Rocky boy. We've gotta silence him."

"What do you mean, silence him?" asked Pumpkin Head.

"Dude, not even Rock here is as stupid as you. Silence, like convince him that he'll be in a world of pain if he doesn't fucking back off."

"And how do we do that?" asked Skinny.

" 'Member how we used to haze the fresh boots?" asked Balls.

"Guys, man, I don't know," said Pumpkin Head.

"Fuck, dude, we all got our blood stripes, right? It's not like we're gonna kill him or anything," said Skinny.

"Right, Skin. We have to do something," said Balls. "It's our duty to fight the terrorists, whether they're in theater or here at home. Now, are we good to go? Whoever isn't better speak up now."

"Man, isn't that kinda John Wayne? I mean, he's not a terrorist, he's a civilian," said Pumpkin Head.

"The enemy comes in all kinds of shapes and sizes. This one even has an ex-FBI poking around where he doesn't belong," said Balls.

"Dude, he talked to me too," said Rock.

"You didn't tell him anything, did you retard?" asked Balls.

"No, man, I swear. I didn't tell him shit. And don't call me retard."

"Guys, this is a threat that has to be taken care of. Are we good to go?"

"Yeah!" they all sung in unison.

"OO RAH!" said Balls, prompting an "OO RAH" from the chorus, and a simultaneous toast of smashing beer mugs.

CHAPTER TWENTY-FIVE

Brent finally got the good news in the mail that his tort claim against the Government was denied. That meant he was free to file the lawsuit, which he had been working on in anticipation of this moment. The past sixty days had turned up no new evidence and no witnesses, but he didn't really expect any. Rick had had the door slammed in his face with every contact.

G. K. Chesterson said, "The true soldier fights not because he hates what is in front of him, but because he loves what is behind him." No matter what had been done to Ahmed, no matter what stomachs had dropped to the boots of however many post-adolescent servicemen; their honor had been inextricably entwined with loyalty without question to their superiors, and they weren't going to talk about the ugly deeds that they had either witnessed or done in the name of service to their country.

It was in this context that Brent threw the gauntlet against George W. Bush, the highest-ranking officer of the American military machine, the same man who had said, "One of the hardest parts of my job is to connect Iraq to the war on terror." After all, a "War on Terror" was an anomaly. How could you have a war on terrorism when war *is* terrorism? Brent was secretly hoping that someone would come to their senses and come forward to keep the stink of war away from home.

The complaint was filed in U.S. District Court in Los Angeles, and announced in a press release, which drew both praise and criticism. Since the habeas corpus case was deemed "related" by the presiding judge, the new case was assigned to Judge Henley. The chat boards were alive with the news of the filing. Some called Brent a "liberal," others "a defender of civil liberties," and others still branded him an "opportunist" or a "terrorist lover."

Stepping forward for something worth believing in is never popular if it goes against the mass hypnosis.

Americans are raised in school pledging allegiance to a flag; they sing the national anthem and feel tingle run up and down their spine when they hear it. Then, when they grow up, they play "follow the leader," complying with every badge of authority flashed at them without question. In what little public discourse they have, they debate the issues of conflict between fictitious characters on television shows and repeat the opinions of media pundits as their own.

It was going to be tough to find a jury who would be sympathetic to a wife and family who had lost a husband accused of terrorism against the United States, and a Muslim one at that.

***

Private Lee Smith, also known as "Pumpkin Head," was running through the jungle in his cammies being chased by a huge tiger. Then he tripped and dropped his piece, leaving himself completely unprotected. No matter how fast he ran, the tiger was still right behind him. He could feel the tiger's breath against his neck, and then the tiger pounced, sat heavily on his chest and bared his teeth for the final kill.

Suddenly Smith awoke in his bunk to Balls' strong hand clamped against his mouth and the gleaming blade of his K-BAR pinned against Smith's throat.

"Did I detect a lack of enthusiasm last night?"

Smith mumbled, and Balls drew back the blade to allow him to shake his head "No."

Balls lifted his hand from Smith's mouth. "If I charge, what do you do?" he asked, removing his grip from Smith's mouth.

"Follow you."

"And if I retreat?"

"Kill you."

"And if I die?"

"Revenge you."

"Good. I don't have to tell you that what happened in Gitmo stays in Gitmo, do I?"

"No Balls, of course not."

"Are you good to go then?"

"Yeah, yeah, I'm good to go."

Balls sheathed his knife and smiled.

∗∗∗

After the complaint was served, Brent served his autopsy report from Dr. Orozco on the U.S. Attorney's office, along with his early disclosures, and made an ex parte emergency motion for expedited discovery. All formal discovery in federal court was normally postponed until after the court holds its first conference, at which time both sides are expected to propose discovery plans. Brent was seeking an order to allow him early discovery.

Brent alleged that the fact that any one of his witnesses could be shipped off for deployment to Iraq or Afghanistan at any time was good cause to allow him to take depositions right away. The motion was granted, and Brent put out notices of deposition on Sergeant Brown, Corporal Reeding and Colonel Masters, all personnel he had met during his Gitmo visits. They were all still on the base in their current deployment, so he would have to make at least one more trip back to Gitmo to depose them.

"Don't expect much," Rick had told him. Brent knew that but he had to start at the tail of the snake to find the head.

The depositions were set by agreement with the U.S. Attorney's office, which had to work with the U.S. Navy to obtain clearance for Brent and Rick. Brent also made a demand to inspect all documents, including the detainee contact logs for Ahmed, any use of force reports, the force-feeding facilities, the cells that held Ahmed Khury during his vacation at Camp 7, the interrogation and recreation facilities, and finally, all leg and arm restraints, belly restraints, black out hoods, ear muffs, and goggles and gloves, which all drew the objection that they were "classified," something Judge Henley quickly threw out when the U.S. Attorney moved for a protective order.

***

As the days neared his "fishing expedition," Brent spent long hours at the office, keeping up with his other cases, so he could afford the week off that it would take to do a thorough job turning Gitmo upside down. News of the discovery trip circulated through the ranks, giving Brent a reputation as a hated man long before he had set foot on Cuban soil.

Brent's routine the week leading to the trip was monk-like. He worked all day and most of the night, preparing for the depositions. He never saw Debbie, who had an annoying habit of calling him at night with nothing to say, and the only time he did get out was to meet with Rick to compare notes.

Brent preferred to walk to his meetings with Rick, which were invariably held in some dive on State Street within a mile of his office, so, when Rick called and asked him to meet him at Sonny's, Rick's favorite bar, Brent locked up the office and headed out on foot at about 11 p.m.

The walk to Sonny's was about ten short blocks, and Brent was programmed on autopilot for it, having done it so many times before. As he approached Ortega Street, a teenage kid on a bicycle came up to him.

"Hey man, could you help me? I'm looking for my dog," he asked Brent.

Brent was a little surprised. "I'm kind of busy right now, but good luck."

"I'm just afraid the coyotes will get him. He's down there," the kid said, as he pointed down the street, "Every time I go near him, he runs away. I just need someone to stay here and catch him if he runs, while I come from the other side and try to get him to come out."

"Okay," said Brent, reluctantly, and phoned Rick to tell him he would be late.

"Let the kid find his own goddamn dog," Rick replied.

"Dude, I'm only three blocks away, come on over, you can help me get it over with."

As Brent waited with his eyes trained on the alley, he was grabbed from behind by two guys.

Brent strained to see his captors, and two more appeared before him in ski masks covering everything but their eyes and mouths. They threw him against the wall in the alley and taped his mouth, hands and feet with duct tape. One of them, the only one who did the talking, whipped out a huge knife. Another cocked and pointed a huge gun right at his head.

"Now listen up, Mr. Lawyer, because there's gonna be a quiz after," said the Talker, who laughed and the other three laughed along in chorus.

"And if you don't get all the questions right, my buddy here is gonna put a bullet in your head. It's only an eighty-cent bullet to us, so pay attention." More laughter.

Brent nodded, his eyes wide open in terror.

"Your case against the Government is going nowhere. Nobody is going to tell you anything, because nothing happened. Do you understand?"

Brent nodded.

"You're messing in shit where you don't belong and you're way out of your league," said the Talker, who ripped the duct tape off Brent's mouth, shoved in a rag, and taped it back over his nose and mouth.

"Am I making myself clear?" Brent nodded, trying not to panic and hoping that Rick would get his ass there, and quickly. Out of the corner of his eye he could see Rick creeping up on them, making the silent "shhh" sign with his finger.

Rick was like a wild animal when he attacked, and disarmed the man with the gun at the same time he kicked the knife out of the Talker's hand: A real James Bond. The Talker tried to rush Rick, but he stood in front of Brent and pointed the gun at all of them back and forth in a semi-circle. "Who wants a piece of this?" he yelled, "Let's see how many of you I can shoot before you get to us." The four ran off in a unison retreat, as Brent turned purple.

Rick quickly ripped the tape off his mouth and Brent coughed and sucked in as much air as he could in one breath.

"You okay, buddy?" he asked, as Rick cut him free from his bonds.

"Good, cause I've gotta go get those motherfuckers." Rick whipped out his cell phone to call his cop buddies.

"Let's get you out in the light. Rick ushered Brent back to State Street. Can you get to Sonny's and wait for me there?" Rick asked, putting his hand on Brent's shoulder.

"Yeah, I'm alright."

"Okay, I'll be back," he said, evoking an image of Schwarzenegger, and ran off, his cell phone attached to his ear.

***

Rick finally got back to Sonny's around 1 a.m. "The trail went cold," he said, "They were probably military or ex- military. The knife is KA-BAR, they call them K-BAR, standard Marine Corps issue. No prints on the handle and I messed up the prints on the gun when I took it to save our asses. Probably our buddies from Gitmo- the same ones I tried to interview."

"I thought Gitmo guards were mostly Army."

"They are, but the ones who guard the base itself are Marines."

"Did you give the cops a list of names?"

"I'm way ahead of you buddy. If any of those assholes are in California, we're going to haul them in."

CHAPTER TWENTY-SIX

The following week Brent and Rick were on a plane to Ft. Lauderdale, and then off to Gitmo for a week of depositions and discovery. Their plane was met by Corporal Lance Peppard, a young 20-something who could have passed for Corporal Reeding. He even had the same Southern drawl.

"Where's Reeding?" asked Brent.

"Oh, he was reassigned months ago, sir."

Rick was shocked at the cloak and dagger methods that were used to keep them from figuring out the location of Camp 7.

"Even if we knew where Camp 7 was, then what?" he asked Peppard through his blackout hood.

"I assume that was rhetorical, sir?"

"Yes, Peppard, don't get your balls in an uproar."

Corporal Peppard took them on a tour of the specific points that were enumerated in the court order. First stop was the cell that Ahmed had lived in the last days of his life. It was a small concrete block with no windows: just a steel door with no bars. Rick took photographs of every detail of the cell. Only one detail was missing: There was no heavy metal music played during the entire tour. The hole where Ahmed spent his days in solitary confinement was even smaller, with no bed, no toilet, and no wire mesh ceiling.

The force-feeding room looked like the bland and plain room that you would expect to find in a medical clinic, the centerpiece of which was the bizarre force-feeding chair, with the hand, foot and head restraints you may expect to find on a chair used for lethal injections or the electric chair.

They examined the two-foot long nasal feeding tubes and gravity feeding bags. The jackpot came when Rick and Brent were given a copy of a video which showed every sickening detail of Ahmed being force-fed, including the presence of the feeding team who had extracted Ahmed from his cell, dressed in full riot gear: bullet proof flak jackets over their camouflage fatigues, helmets with visors. Brent and Rick watched in horror the 25-minute-long video, which showed Ahmed being strapped in the chair, screaming in pain as the tube was inserted into his nostril without anesthesia, coughing and spitting out the tube twice, and finally vomiting blood after the feeding.

"Is this the only video of Mr. Khury being force -fed?" asked Brent.

"Yes sir," replied Corporal Peppard.

The tour finished in the TV room, where detainees were shackled to the floor to watch television, the interrogation room, with its four blank walls and the post in the floor to shackle detainees' arms and legs in a fetal position while they were being interrogated, the shower room, where detainees are allowed one 15-minute shower per week, and finally, the exercise area, a 10-five by eight foot chain link structure, like a small dog run, with multiple fences and loads of barbed wire, where Camp 7 detainees are allowed 15 minutes of "exercise" per week.

***

"Dude, that place is a Gulag," said Rick, as they sat in the 'House of Yum,' exhausted both physically and emotionally. "They've got this McDonald's and KFC on the outside, total Americana, right? And they're right next door to the House of Pain."

"Write a letter to your Congressman, Rick," said Brent, facetiously.

"No, seriously, they say you're a terrorist, ship you off to a U.S. base and do anything they want to you because you're technically not in America? That's gotta be a crime."

"The president's legal advisors don't think so. They say the Geneva Conventions don't apply to detainees, and neither does their own Military Code of Justice."

"Dude, we could never get away with that shit in the States."

"Yes they can," said Brent. "Thanks to the Patriot Act, they can secretly raid your house, eavesdrop on your email, and grab your private banking and library records. They can look up your online asshole with a microscope using their 'roving warrant.' They can hold you on no charges for up to five days, and, if you're an immigrant, indefinitely."

"It's not right."

"That's why we're here. This is not the greatest vacation destination, you know?"

CHAPTER TWENTY-SEVEN

Depositions are usually tedious and boring. They are a discovery tool which allows the attorney taking the deposition to ask more than he would at the time of trial, because there is no judge present to rule on objections, which are mostly for the record, to be decided upon at trial if the transcript of the deposition is used for something. Even if a witness was lying, you can get a good indication of his demeanor as a witness at trial.

Rick Penn's presence was invaluable to Brent, as he was an expert at reading facial expressions and body language. He was the closest thing to a human polygraph machine.

The deposition of Sergeant William Brown promised to be a most difficult one. The deposition took place inside a conference room at Camp Delta, the likes Brent had never seen before at Camp 7. It had a classic wooden conference table, with padded chairs, an American flag, of course, and pictures of George W. Bush and Dick Cheney on the walls.

Brown was represented by a JAG naval officer, as well as the Assistant U.S. Attorney from the DOJ's Los Angeles office, Timothy Nagel, a wiry looking young nerd with 70's style glasses and a baggy suit, whom Brent supposed was going to be more of a challenge than he looked.

The festivities started right away, when Brent and Rick sat down across from Brown.

"Who is this man?" asked Nagel.

"This is my investigator," replied Brent.

"He can't be in here."

"Okay, let's break and go to Los Angeles to hear a motion on your protective order. See you back here tomorrow. Deposition adjourned."

"Wait a minute, wait a minute. I guess it's okay," Nagel relented.

The deposition of Brown proved to be all that Brent thought it would. He was well coached, and instructed not to answer questions that were considered "classified." His testimony was, for the most part, given in a dry, emotionless monotone. However, when Brent went into unchartered territory, the fishing got a little bit better.

"Sergeant Brown, is there an operating procedure for processing new detainees at Camp 7?"

"Yes, sir."

"Are you trained on those procedures?"

"There is manual of standard operating procedures."

"Mr. Nagel, will you agree to produce the manual without a motion?"

"It's classified."

"Was Mr. Khury processed as a new detainee at Camp 7 in accordance with the standard operating procedure?"

"Yes, sir."

"And can you describe his processing?"

"Objection, irrelevant."

"Go ahead, Sergeant," said Brent.

"Counsel, this isn't relevant to your wrongful death claim."

"It may lead to the discovery of admissible evidence, so I'm entitled to it. Are you instructing him not to answer? Shall we break for a motion to compel?"

"No, but I reserve the right to do so, depending on the question."

"Fair enough. Sergeant Brown, please describe the procedure of how Mr. Khury was processed as a new detainee."

"Well, upon arrival, he was cleaned, his clothes disposed of, personal property bagged and accounted for, earmuffs and black boxes removed for return to the Air Force, and hand and ankle shackles replaced with our standard issue."

"What was the next step of processing?"

Brown looked at Nagel, and at the JAG for any disapproval, and, seeing none, continued.

"He was then cleaned, his hair cut, and was strip searched."

"Did this include a body cavity search?"

"Yes, sir."

"Then what?"

"The next step of processing was to implement a Phase One Behavior Management Plan as directed by the JIG."

"What is the JIG?"

"Joint Interrogation Group."

"What did you do to implement the Phase One Behavior Management Plan on Mr. Khury?"

"First, he was given his basic comforts-only package."

"What was in the basic comforts-only package?"

"An ISO mat, one blanket, one towel, one roll of toilet paper, toothpaste and a finger toothbrush, one Styrofoam cup, one bar of soap, a copy of the camp rules, and a Koran."

"What kind of contact was allowed Mr. Khury during Phase One of his behavior management plan?"

"No contact."

"Not even the International Red Cross?"

"No, sir."

"What if he had a medical problem?"

"He didn't."

"Was he given access to reading material?"

"No, sir."

"How long did Phase One last?"

"Two weeks."

"Was there a Phase Two of behavior management?"

"Yes, sir."

"What did Phase Two consist of?"

"Phase Two was a program to isolate Mr. Khury and foster his dependence on the interrogators."

"How was that done?"

"By exploiting his sense of disorientation and disorganization."

"And who was the interrogator?"

"Objection, that is classified," said Nagel.

"Join," said the JAG.

"I intend to schedule an Order to Show Cause why the identity of the interrogator be kept secret, and an order allowing me to depose him," said Brent.

"Go ahead," said Nagel. "It's classified."

"How was he isolated?"

"He was kept in an isolation cell in the MSU."

"With no windows?"

"Correct."

"What is the MSU?"

"Maximum Security Unit."

"Was the cell lit?"

"As needed."

"What does that mean?" asked Brent.

"It was lit per the instructions of the JIG."

"Was Mr. Khury subject to long periods of blackout?"

"What do you mean by blackout, sir?"

"Long periods of time with no light in his isolation cell."

"I don't remember."

"How long was Mr. Khury in isolation?"

"Four weeks."

"Was Mr. Khury classified as *a non-privileged enemy combatant*?"

"Yes, sir."

"By whom?"

"The JIG."

"What is your definition of torture, Sergeant Brown?"

"That which inflicts serious pain, likely to be experienced by great bodily injury, such as the destruction of an organ."

"Is that definition something you made up yourself?"

"No, sir. It's SOP."

"Standard Operating Procedure?"

"Yes, sir."

"Do you know what waterboarding is, Sergeant?"

"Yes, sir."

"Was Mr. Khury ever waterboarded?"

"No, sir," said Brown, furrowing his brows.

"Do you know what dry-boarding is?"

"Yes, sir," said Brown, tensing up.

"Was Mr. Khury ever dry-boarded?"

"No, sir," he replied, blinking and scratching his nose.

* * *

"That motherfucker's lying," said Rick, after the day long deposition, as they soothed their tattered nerves with a couple of brews at O'Kelly's Irish Pub with their favorite escort Colonel Peppard looking on from the end of the bar.

"About what?"

"Waterboarding. Did you see him furrow his brows?"

"Yeah, so?"

"Alone, that micro-expression is not foolproof, but he also moved his eyes from up and to the right."

"And when he talked about dry-boarding, he went into a blinking fit."

"I noticed that."

"We've got the nurse tomorrow. That's when I'm really gonna need your lie detection skills."

171

"You can count on it."

As they spoke, Corporal Reeding bellied up to the bar. Brent waved to him, and he waved back. Corporal Reeding approached Peppard, and Rick and Brent came closer for introductions.

"I hope he's treating you well, Mr. Marks," said Reeding.

"He is, Corporal. Very well. This is my investigator, Rick Penn.

Penn put out his hand to Reeding, who took it with a firm grip.

"Good to meet you," said Reeding, then went back to pick up his beer at the other end of the bar.

Back at the tent, Brent and Rick were provided for their overnight stay, Rick opened his hand to show what Corporal Reeding had secretly pressed into it. He pointed to it and gave the "shh" sign with his finger.

Brent unfolded the paper and they both read, *I need to speak with you, but it's impossible to do here. Will be on leave starting next week in Miami. Too dangerous to use phones. Can you meet me at the Colony Hotel in South Beach on Monday at 2100 hrs?*

"It just keeps getting weirder and weirder." said Brent. Since they didn't feel free to speak about this latest event, Rick kept the note for safekeeping, to be discussed as soon as they were away from the base.

CHAPTER TWENTY-EIGHT

The deposition of James Benson, the U.S. Navy nurse, was a rehearsed set of "I don't recalls." It was not very helpful, but interesting nevertheless because he was sweating profusely and looked very uncomfortable in his seat.

"Are you feeling alright, Nurse Benson?" asked Brent.

"Yes, sir. I'm fine. I've never been through this procedure before."

"You understand, I'm not here to trick you – just to find out what you know about the case— don't you?"

"Yes, sir."

"You were the nurse who last fed Mr. Khury before his suicide, is that correct?"

"Yes sir."

Nurse Benson went through the procedure used for the feeding, including the restraint of Ahmed, and the preparation of his feeding tube.

"Was the feeding tube lubricated?"

"Yes, sir."

"With what?"

"Olive oil. That was his choice."

"Is olive oil an approved lubricant for enteral feeding?"

"Yes, sir."

"By whom is it approved?"

"By my command, by SOUTHCOM."

"Then what did you do?"

"I asked the detainee what flavor of Ensure he wanted."

"You mean, you asked Mr. Khury that?"

"Yes, sir."

"Did that make sense to you, Nurse Benson, that if the product was being delivered straight to his stomach, how would he be able to taste it?"

"We were required to give him the choice."

"I see. Then what happened?"

"I asked him if he wanted to play a video game during the procedure."

"Did he?"

"No."

"Did you expect him to?"

"Many of the detainees ask to play video games."

"What did you do next?"

"I inserted the lubricated feeding tube into his nostril and then commenced the feeding," said the nurse, as he wiped sweat from his brow. He looked flushed.

"Were there any complications?"

"No, sir."

"Did Mr. Khury complain about anything?"

"Yes, sir. He said the tube felt strange, but they always say that."

"They always say that?"

"Yes, sir." The nurse gulped, then nodded.

"Did he say why it felt strange?"

"No, but he did cough up the tube." The nurse smacked his dry lips, and then cleared his throat.

"Does that happen often?"

"Sometimes."

"Then what happened?"

"The detainee was taken back to his cell."
The nurse leaned back in his chair, fidgeting.

"By whom?"

"Sergeant Brown."

***

In the break, Rick consulted with Brent in
the men's room.

"He's lying."

"About what?"

"Everything except the choice of flavors and
olive oil."

"He did look a bit flustered."

"A bit flustered? Dude, it was like you were
force-feeding *him*!"

***

After the break, Brent went straight for the kill. He wasn't going to get anything from this witness, so the best he could do was try to show that he was lying, and to plant the seed of the truth in the jurors' minds.

"Nurse Benson, do you know of the term, 'aspiration?'"

Benson fidgeted in his seat and scratched at his neck.

"Yes, sir."

"You know that Mr. Khury was found dead the day after his enteral feeding, do you not?"

"Yes, sir."

"Isn't it true, Nurse Benson that, during his enteral feeding, Mr. Khury aspirated his liquid Ensure?"

"No, sir," said Benson, going for a glass of water and sipping it, hands shaking like an 80-year-old with Parkinson's.

"Isn't it true, sir, that Mr. Khury became unconscious during his feeding?"

"No, sir." The beads of sweat were popping out on Benson's forehead as if he had been in a sauna for half an hour.

"Isn't it true, sir that you attempted to revive Mr. Khury, and were unsuccessful?"

"No sir!" Benson answered, raising the volume of his voice.

"And that Mr. Khury died in the feeding chair?"

"No sir!"

"You checked for his pulse, didn't you Nurse Benson?"

"Objection, asked and answered," said Nagel.

"No sir!"

"It's not your fault, Benson, but you do have to tell the truth," Brent insisted.

"Objection argumentative!"

"Tell the truth Benson, or you'll never be able to live with yourself!"

"I am telling the truth!"

"There is no question pending," said Nagel. I'm instructing the witness to say no more to this line of questioning."

"Join," said the JAG.

"Oh, I'm not finished yet," said Brent.

"Who removed Mr. Khury from the feeding chair?"

"Corporal Reeding and Sergeant Brown," said Benson.

"When did Sergeant Brown come in?"

"He was called by Corporal Reeding?"

"What for?"

"Calls for speculation," said the JAG.

"Corporal Reeding became nervous when the detainee coughed out the feeding tube."

"The detainee had a name, didn't he Benson?"

"Yes, sir."

"Does it make you feel better, calling him "the detainee" instead of by name, like a human being?"

"The witness will not answer that question," instructed Nagel.

CHAPTER TWENTY-NINE

Corporal Brian Reeding's deposition proved to be a bit smoother than the others. But what he was not telling festered on Brent like a mosquito bite that you can't stop scratching. Reeding's body language was point-on, according to Rick. So what could he be hiding?

"What compelled you to call Sergeant Brown during Mr. Khury's feeding?"

"Mr. Khury was complaining that the feeding tube was hurting him and he subsequently coughed up the tube."

"Did you think that he might be in danger?"

"I thought he might be, yes, sir."

"And how many of these force-feedings had you been present at before this one?"

"Objection to the characterization of the feeding as a force-feeding," said the JAG.

"It was a new detail for me, so not that many, but enough that this one made me alarmed."

"And what happened after Brown arrived?"

"He cleared the room."

"What do you mean by 'cleared the room?"

"He sent my team out."

"Including you?"

"Yes."

"And what did your team do?"

"Sergeant Brown ordered the team to secure the next detainee for feeding."

"And Nurse Benson and Sergeant Brown remained in the feeding room?"

"Yes, sir."

On cross-examination, Nagel did his best to destroy the credibility of Corporal Reeding.

"Corporal, you testified that this was a new detail for you, is that correct?"

"Yes, sir."

"And isn't it true that you have no medical background?"

"Yes, sir."

"So you don't know that Mr. Khury was in danger when you observed him coughing up the feeding tube, isn't that correct?"

"He looked like he was."

"But you can't say for a fact that he was in any kind of a bodily crisis as a result of the procedure, isn't that correct?"

"No sir, I can't."

"And isn't it true that Mr. Khury told you that he wanted to die?"

"Yes, sir."

"How many times did you hear him say that?"

"Several times."

***

The depositions of the feeding team were like playing back the dry recorded voices of a computer using a synthetic speech system. No emotion, no body language, like each one of them had been as programmed as they had been desensitized to the entire force-feeding process. Yes, they had seen many detainees complain about the procedure. Yes, they had seen many of them cough up vomit and blood and still live to tell about it. The entire exercise at trial would come down to the credibility of Brown and Benson as witnesses, and the battle of Dr. Orozco v. the military doctor who would be called as an expert.

Brent and Rick left Gitmo on this note, a bit dejected, but still determined to keep up the fight. The unknown lay ahead, and they were dedicated to making as much of it known as they could.

CHAPTER THIRTY

Being in South Beach, Miami was like stepping back in a time machine to the Art Deco 1950's. It was hot during the day, and equally hot at night, blazing with the neon that the Las Vegas Strip had long forgotten. At 9 p.m., the strip was just warming up, with diners packed in the sidewalk cafés in front of the boutique hotels, being hounded by homeless graduates selling red roses wrapped individually in cellophane and street musicians singing *Besame Mucho* and *La Bamba*.

Brent and Rick found Corporal Reeding sitting at a corner table in front of the Colony Hotel, dressed in his Bermuda shorts and a T-shirt, sipping on a margarita on the rocks. After the mandatory round of handshaking, Rick and Brent joined him.

Smalltalk was cut short by curiosity, however, and, for Brent, every additional second of waiting seemed like an excruciating hour.

"You said you wanted to talk to us," said Brent.

"I do, but only under conditions of confidentiality. How does it work? Can I be a confidential informant?"

"We can talk confidentially now, of course," said Brent. "But if you're implicated at all in any wrongdoing against our client, that's where all confidentiality would cease."

"Oh no, sir, nothing like that."

"Alright then, speak confidentially and tell us what you know."

"I just want to say that I'm very proud to be a soldier and even more proud to be an American. But it's just not right what they're doing down there in Gitmo, it's downright un-American if you ask me."

"What do you mean?"

"I mean, I've done two tours, one in Afghanistan and one in Iraq. We all learn in basic that there's a certain way to act toward your prisoner, and this ain't it, I can tell you that."

"What are they doing that you think is not right?"

"This is anonymous, right? I don't want to be the next guy swinging from the ceiling in my quarters."

"Yes, anonymous."

"Waterboarding, dry-boarding, fake executions, beatings, you name it, they do it. Some guys get used to it, but I can't. I just follow orders."

"Have you thought about reporting this?"

"To who? I'm only talking to you guys because I know you're on the right side. I can't trust anyone, not in my position."

Corporal Reeding continued to describe the house of horrors that was Camp 7: every inhuman act, every violation of the Constitution, the Military Code of Justice and the Geneva Conventions of 1949 that would throw every conviction of every accused who ever set foot in Camp 7 out of court.

"Corporal Reeding?" asked Brent.

"Yes, sir?"

"What really happened in that feeding room to Ahmed?"

"I don't know sir, really I don't. I told you everything I know in my deposition. The only ones who really know are Sergeant Brown and Nurse Benson. And…"

"And who else?"

"I don't know, sir. But I think something went really wrong in that feeding room and they're trying to cover it up."

***

"Those a-holes have fucked up every case against every real terrorist, haven't they?" asked Rick, slamming a shot of whiskey.

"I'm afraid they have," replied Brent, "It's a shame that the guilty ones are going to get off, but that's what happens when you try to change 200 years of checks and balances."

"So, are we gonna stay here awhile and catch some strip acts?"

Brent just gave Rick a look that obviated the need to respond verbally.

"What? Okay, I get it, back to work."

"Back to work," said Brent.

CHAPTER THIRTY-ONE

Corporal Reeding was determined to enjoy his R&R no matter what. He had done his good deed, and now his conscience could have a well-needed rest. Bootsie's Cabaret was just the ticket. Reeding started on the lower level. The main stage was good, the girls were hot and the beer was cold. He grabbed a pile of fresh $1 bills from his pocket and folded them in little tents in front of himself on the bright red stage to entice the chicks to give him the closest view of their very best features.

A knockout blonde with green eyes was his object of attention. His gaze was glued on her with fascination as she did her final act, completely nude. She jumped on the pole in the center of the stage, slinked up as high as the ceiling, and then glided down backwards into a perfect split. When she came to pick up his collection of $1 bills, she smiled at Reeding and blew him a kiss.

During the next act, the blonde came up to Reeding and asked him if he wanted to go to the VIP Room. Of course he did.

"How much does it cost?"

"$20 for a lap dance, $300 for full service."

"What's a full service include?"

"Everything."

"Let's go for the lap dance."

In the blue-lit glow of a little alcove of the VIP Room, Blondie gyrated her privates against Reeding's stiffening member, then reached around with her hand and started to rub it. Then the third song had finished.

"Time's up!"

"No!"

"Full service?" she whispered, as she squeezed it again. Reeding, his judgment already impaired with alcohol and long-term horniness, succumbed, and she led him to a private booth in the back of the VIP Room.

＊

While Reeding was getting his reward for his honesty, back on the main floor, three crew cuts came in and joined the fourth at the main stage.

"Where is he?" asked Balls.

"He's upstairs in the VIP Room, getting a lap dance," said Skinny.

"Don't you guys fuck this up like you did in California," said Balls.

"Don't worry," said Skinny. "He won't even know what hit him."

As Reeding stumbled down the stairs with a goofy grin on his face, he didn't notice the four amigos at all. Reeding navigated a wavy course through the smoke filled room of too many guys, and went out the door.

The four followed. It was too easy. Skinny and Pumpkin Head slipped ahead of Reeding to scout for an alley to slip into, while Balls and Rock followed him. Once Balls saw that Skinny and Pumpkin Head had themselves tucked away in a dark alley, Balls gave the order and he and Rock slipped on their masks and pushed Reeding into the alley.

"You've got a big mouth," said Balls.

"What, what are you talking about?" slurred Reeding. "Who are you guys?"

"You'd better learn how to keep it shut or next time you won't be so lucky."

Reeding was tipped to the opposite scale of the soft pleasure he had just experienced as the four beat him into an unconscious blob.

CHAPTER THIRTY-TWO

Benjamin Franklin said, "Justice will not be served until those who are unaffected are as outraged as those who are." The U.S. Military had become the strong right arm of an over-zealous president and his cabinet. The next six months were a struggle to obtain documents, records and identify witnesses who were all deemed by the military to be "classified."

Judge Henley, not wanting to be branded as partial, since he had already granted Ahmed's habeas corpus petition, split the baby. He granted roughly half of Brent's motions, and denied the other half, on the grounds that the material requested was sensitive to national security and did not lead to the discovery of admissible evidence in Brent's case.

Brent and Rick spent long hours at the office. Rick put together witness lists and exhibits, and worked with Melinda to organize them, and Brent worked on the trial brief, opening statement to the jury, and his witness outlines, until, finally, the pretrial conference was upon them.

"These are the times that try men's souls," said Rick.

"You know who coined that phrase?"

"Who?"

"Thomas Paine."

"Another great American."

"Yes, we are stepping into the shoes of many great ones who have gone before us," said Brent.

***

At the pre-trial, Judge Henley laid down the rules of his courtroom for the jury trial. There would be no surprises. Everything had already been disclosed and exhibits exchanged. It would be as fair a fight as possible, and, despite the huge disparity between the two sides in terms of power and money, Brent was comfortable on his side of the courtroom because when it came to argument, no amount of money and power could triumph over the power of the spoken word.

Brent would make the jury see what Ahmed saw, to feel what Ahmed felt. The theory of his case was twofold: either they were negligent in the feeding procedure, causing Ahmed's death, or the alternative, if it was more palatable to the jury, that Ahmed was psychologically broken to the point of suicide and they were negligent in not taking precautions for his safety. The alternative theory allowed Brent to bring in all the evidence of the treatment that the Government did not define as "torture." The jury would give that treatment its own definition, and it would be broadcast to the masses. The trial would begin in two weeks.

PART III

A PATRIOT'S ACT

CHAPTER THIRTY-THREE

The closest thing to a jury trial would probably be live theater. Luckily, Brent had been able to sleep well the night before the trial; something that he wasn't always able to do. He had spent many a night before a trial worrying about it, and going over it in his mind. No matter how well prepared he was, he seemed to always feel like he was missing something. But when he was in the heat of battle, he carried himself confidently and well.

Brent put the finishing touches on his appearance, which was more important than anything else on the first day. He had to exude confidence, but not give the appearance of being vain. He had laid out his suit the night before; a classic navy blue Cerruti. As he tied the Windsor knot of his dark blue tie on the collar of his teleprompter blue shirt, the image of the actor was complete.

**

Brent met Catherine in the parking lot, so they could walk into the courthouse together. No matter how early they could have planned to be, they would never have avoided the crowds.

A small group of protestors holding signs saying, "Close Guantanamo" and "Gitmo has to go" gathered on the sidewalk across from the courthouse, along with five people dressed in orange jumpsuits with black hoods. An opposing group holding "Remember 911" signs and signs that read, "Death to Terrorists" shouted at the demonstrators from their spot on the corner about 100 meters away. It was folly for the news crews and reporters, who swarmed around Brent and Catherine like a bunch of bees fishing for comments, but there could be no talking to the media yet. The case came first.

Inside the courtroom, the usual humdrum, quiet pace was a welcome change to the circus outside. Brent and Catherine took a seat and waited for the judge to take the bench.

*** *** ***

"Catherine Khury v. George W. Bush, et. al, case Number CV 08 – 36749. Counsel, please state your appearances."

"Good morning, Your Honor. Brent Marks appearing for the Plaintiff, Catherine Khury."

"Good morning, Mr. Marks."

"Good morning, Your Honor. Assistant U.S. Attorney Timothy Nagel for the Government."

"Good morning, Mr. Nagel."

"Good morning, Your Honor. Assistant U.S. Attorney Joseph Cicatto for the Government."

"Good morning, Mr. Cicatto. Call in the first panel, please, Madame Clerk."

A panel of jurors shuffled in, and Judge Henley identified the parties and witnesses, to make sure that none of the jurors knew any of them, proceeding to question the jurors as to their names, where they lived, their marital status and education. Then he handed the show over to the lawyers.

Representing the Plaintiff, Brent had the first opportunity for *voir dire,* the preliminary questioning that each lawyer would do to determine if any of the jurors had any biases that could hurt (or help) their respective cases. It also gave the opportunity to do a little foreshadowing of the case that lay ahead.

Brent had already read the jury questionnaires of each prospective juror, and Rick had done a background check on all of them. There was nothing alarming, just a group of middle-class folks of all ages and backgrounds with only one thing in common: None of them wanted to be sitting in the jury box.

Brent started the *voir dire* with a little show and tell. He held up a large headshot of Ahmed for the potential jurors to see. "Tell me who you see in the photograph." he asked Dominic Petrelli, an assembly line worker at the Toyota manufacturing plant.

"It looks like an Arab guy," responded Petrelli. The same question was posed to each member in the panel, and Brent made a note of their responses on the "juror map" on his desk, in which he had written the names of all the jurors in the panel.

Each side would have a total of three peremptory challenges to potential jurors, not a lot compared to the six given each side under California law. The challenges would have to be used wisely. Sometimes, believe it or not, the other side disliked a potential juror as much as Brent did. Brent elicited responses from the entire panel on the photograph and received three "Arab" responses. That would make his exercise of the challenges tricky.

Nagel did not waste any time planting the seed of terrorism in the jury's mind.

"Who in the jury box remembers what happened to our country on September 11th, 2001?" There was a unanimous show of hands. *Of course! Who didn't?*

"Juror No. 12, Mr. Steelman, do you believe that our president was correct when he announced to the nation that the United States would win the War on Terror on September 11th?"

"Yes, of course I do."

"Now by a show of hands, who thinks that President Bush was right to go after the Taliban in Afghanistan for harboring al Qaeda?" Every one of the prospective jurors raised their hand. All Nagel needed was a flag in his hand to waive while he made his speech.

"Do you think it was right for the Congress to give the president authorization to use military force against whom the president determined to be responsible for the September 11th attacks and the countries who harbored them?" Again, all hands went up.

And now the ten-million-dollar question.

"Do you feel that it is necessary and proper for every citizen to make sacrifices in the name of the War on Terror so that everyone in our nation can be safe from terrorism?" This time two jurors did not raise their hands. These were the two that Nagel would kick off the jury. Brent would be hard pressed to get a jury in this case that would be sympathetic to a woman who lost a husband who was an accused terrorist.

The tedious questioning of the panel continued for about an hour, with the time divided equally between Brent and Nagel. Finally, their initial time, which had been set by the Court, was up.

"The Court will hear any challenges for cause," said Judge Henley.

"Pass for cause, Your Honor," said Brent.

"Pass for cause, Your Honor," said Nagel.

"Alright then, the first peremptory challenge is with the Plaintiff."

"The Plaintiff wishes to thank and excuse Juror No. 1, Mr. Dominic Petrelli."

Petrelli was excused, and the clerk drew another potential juror's name from the gallery, filling Petrelli's seat.

"The next peremptory challenge is with the Defendant."

"The Defendant wishes to thank and excuse Juror No. 4, Javier Manuel."

This was a blow to Brent, who wanted to keep as many ethnic jurors on the panel as possible. Nagel, of course, wanted only whites.

Finally, after the process was repeated for the new prospective jurors and each party had exercised their three peremptory challenges, the show was ready to begin. The final jury was comprised of one African-American man, one Mexican-American man, three white women and seven white men.

"Madame Clerk, please swear in the jury," instructed Judge Henley. The swearing was followed by the traditional admonishments, prohibiting the jurors from talking to anyone about the case, even amongst themselves, then gave them all a well- deserved lunch break.

CHAPTER THIRTY-FOUR

"Our country has been faced with many different challenges in our lifetime," said Brent, making eye contact with each juror separately as he made his opening statement.

"When we were attacked on September 11th, 2001, we were *all* attacked. Everyone in this room has the right to feel violated, to feel shock, depression, even anger." With each emotion, Brent expressed his own, which came naturally. Even though he disagreed with the president, it was difficult to listen to George W. Bush's post-9/11 speech without feeling a shiver.

"But we mustn't let those emotions and the fever for revenge make us forget what made our nation so great, and that everything that we stand for that was attacked on September 11th. We are a nation of laws: laws that were designed to protect each and every one of us, and the highest form of our law is embodied in the United States Constitution, which has worked well for us for over 200 years. Ladies and Gentlemen, in this trial, you are the guardians of that Constitution. Once we decide on a course of action that deviates from the law, we become the criminals.

"Theodore Roosevelt once said, "No man is justified in doing evil on the ground of expediency." It is only by respecting the law that we can bring justice to any criminal. Benjamin Franklin said, "Those who can give up essential liberty to obtain a little temporary safety deserve neither liberty nor safety." It is you who will decide whether it is right to discard the Constitution and wave the flag as we charge into battle, or to wrap yourself in the Constitution and still wave the flag in support of your country being the most fair and most free country in the world, a beacon of justice for every other free world country to look up to."

"Objection, Your Honor, argumentative," barked Nagel.

"Overruled. Please continue, Mr. Marks."

"Thank you, Your Honor. It was Winston Churchill who said, "The power of the executive to cast a man into prison without formulating any charge known to the law and particularly to deny him the judgment of his peers is in the highest degree odious and is the foundation of all totalitarian government, whether Nazi or Communist." Some of you were born here, and some of you are naturalized American citizens. The Plaintiff, Catherine Khury was married to a naturalized American citizen.

"Ahmed Khury was a loving husband, a father, and a good provider for his family. But, one day, when he was coming to the aid of his brother in his native Iraq, he was captured by the United States military, for suspicion of aiding and abetting his brother in money laundering. Without charge, he was held in Guantanamo Bay Detention Camp for almost a year: A year without being allowed to see or speak to his family. A year in which he endured some of the most unspeakable acts of cruelty ever committed by one human being against another, all sanctioned by the U.S. military. Acts that we intend to show violated the Constitution, the Military Code of Justice, the Torture Conventions and the Geneva Conventions of 1949.

"Ahmed was granted a writ of habeas corpus, which means that the Government was compelled to free him. But, instead of being freed, Ahmed died in Guantanamo. We intend to present evidence, in the form of testimony and documentation, that the Government was responsible for Ahmed's death.

Brent paused, lowered his head halfway to the podium, and then raised it back up, checking to see whether or not he still had the jury. All eyes were on him, and he continued. They listened to Brent as if they were watching a movie, as he drew a picture he intended to paint with the evidence, despite the frequent objections by Nagel to throw him off.

"You will hear the testimony of military personnel at Guantanamo, who will testify that Ahmed talked of suicide. You will hear them testify that they found him hanging dead from the ceiling of his cell. The Plaintiff will present evidence of our version of what happened to Ahmed. Military personnel will testify that he was being force-fed by a military nurse. Dr. Jaime Orozco, an expert pathologist, will testify that the nurse committed medical malpractice and that Ahmed's death was caused by drowning on the liquid nutrients he was being fed because of improper insertion of the feeding tube. The Defendant's expert doctor will testify otherwise.

"You, Ladies and Gentlemen, will be asked to decide, from listening to the evidence, which version of the story is correct. But, it doesn't stop there. If you decide to accept the Government's version that Ahmed committed suicide, then we intend to present evidence to show that this man was psychologically broken by his captors, and tortured mentally and physically to the point that would have driven any human being to suicide to escape the pain of his captivity. And we intend to show that the Government knew the extent of Ahmed's tortured soul, knew that he was driven to suicide by his captors, and did nothing to protect him from his fate.

"Ronald Reagan said, "Our natural and inalienable rights are now considered to be a dispensation from government, and freedom has never been so fragile, so close to slipping through our grasp as it is at this moment." Abraham Lincoln said, "Do not interfere with anything in the Constitution. That must be maintained, for it is the only safeguard of our liberties.""

"Objection, Your Honor!"

"Sustained. The jury will disregard the quotes of our esteemed presidents as argumentative. The time to argue, Mr. Marks, is at the end of the case, not the beginning. Please stick to the facts you intend to outline in your case."

"I will, Your Honor. You will hear evidence about how agents of the FBI broke into Catherine Khury's home, confiscated some of her most precious personal possessions, and eavesdropped on her personal telephone calls

213

and emails, under the authority of the USA Patriot Act. We intend to prove that these were denials of her constitutional civil liberties without allowing her due process under the law, which no act of any government, even an Act of Congress, is permitted to deny, no matter what the circumstances."

＊

The trial skills of Timothy Nagel were undeniable as he gave his opening statement.

"Ladies and Gentlemen, I agree with Mr. Marks on one point and one point only: We live in very trying times. The War on Terror is perhaps the most difficult war we have ever waged. But it is a war, and in a war, we can't pretend that it is business as usual and that no one is going to get hurt.

"Nobody wants war, but when the United States was attacked, our president had no choice but to defend each and every one of you. Our Congress authorized the president to use military force, to seek out and find the perpetrators of this heinous crime and to bring them to justice.

"No war comes without a change in the way things are done. In order for the military to do their job, they have to do things that none of us would ever do. They have to seek out and kill the enemy. As the president said, "It is either us, or them." We have seen, in this enemy, unspeakable evil: To wage war against innocent men, women and children, not in the battlefield, but in our homes and our offices. This cannot be tolerated.

"In such cases of battling terrible evil, we all have to make sacrifices for the common good. My able opponent has made use of the quotations of great men in his opening remarks. It was Winston Churchill who also said, "Never, never, believe that any war will be smooth and easy, or that anyone who embarks on the strange voyage can measure the tides and hurricanes he will encounter." Dwight Eisenhower said, "We are going to have peace even if we have to fight for it." This is an inevitable fact of human existence.

"The enemy of the War on Terror is al Qaeda. My opponent will point out that al Qaeda is not a country, but, Ladies and Gentlemen, it is an organized enemy force nonetheless. Al Qaeda has aligned itself with an enemy government of a foreign nation. The United States Congress gave the authority to our president to seek out al Qaeda and bring its members, as well as the nations harboring them, to justice, such as the Taliban.

"This authorization gives the president the right to detain anyone suspected of being an al Qaeda operative, and the evidence will show that there was overwhelming reason to believe that was the case with Mr. Khury. In such trying times of fighting such enduring enemies of evil, military commissions have been called into play to dispense justice. Just as the war criminals of the Nazi regime were captured, held and tried by military commissions, so is the process that has been set up to handle the terrorists who seek to destroy our way of life."

Brent carefully watched the jury as Nagel gave his speech. They seemed every bit as fascinated with his presentation as they were with Brent's, if not more so.

"As the judge will instruct you, the United States Supreme Court has held that, 'the detention of individuals who have fought against the United States for the duration of the particular conflict in which they are captured, is so fundamental and accepted an incident to war as to be an exercise of the necessary and proper force that Congress has authorized the president to use, and that there is no bar to this nation holding one of its own citizens as an enemy combatant.'

"With regard to allegations of torture, the Government will present evidence that only the most humane and acceptable of methods were used in interrogation and housing of Mr. Khury, all approved by the highest of authority of the US Government.

"The defense will show that Mr. Khury had expressed feelings of suicide, and was offered treatment and medication, all of which he refused. We will offer evidence that he refused food, and was put on a nourishment program to keep him alive. Testimony of the nurse and attendants in this program will be offered to show that the procedures were medically sound, and followed with the utmost of due care.

"Finally, the searches of Mr. Khury's home and personal communications were authorized by amendments to the USA Patriot Act, an Act that has not been struck down by any court of law: An Act which was authorized by Congress itself, in response to the threats of terrorism facing our country."

The jurors had now had their first taste of the case. What followed would be an endless stream of testimony and documents, some of which they would pay attention to, some of which would confuse them, some of which they would daydream through, and others that would pass completely over their heads. In the end, it would come down to emotions, feelings, and the preconceived set of biases and prejudices that they had each had for years. Nothing in the trial would change any of that. Some witnesses would lie, some would tell the truth. What really happened and what didn't really happen would not be important. It would come down, ultimately, to who were the "bad guys" and who were the "good guys." Whoever the jury thought were the "good guys" were going to win. And that decision would not be known for at least ten days.

CHAPTER THIRTY-FIVE

The first witness in the trial was Catherine Khury. In order to paint a picture of a beloved family man, instead of just the "Arab" that the jurors saw in *voir dire*, Catherine would have to tell the story of her husband and their life together, and make him come to life for the jury. Only then could they feel pity for her and her family and realize the full extent of her loss. Only then would they start to care about Catherine and her two small children.

"Mrs. Khury, how old are you?"

"I'm 35 years old."

"When did you and Ahmed get married?"

"We were married 10 years ago, when I was 25."

"Have you ever been married before?"

"No."

"How would you describe your marriage with Ahmed?"

"He was my whole world, the father of my children. I can't imagine living without him," she sobbed, "I'm sorry."

Catherine reached for a Kleenex, and dabbed her tearing eyes. The women of the jury looked at her with compassion.

"Tell us about your children."

Catherine managed to smile at the thought of her children. "Karen's our first-born. She has my eyes, but Ahmed's intelligence and patience. I can see him in her mannerisms sometimes. She's very much to herself a lot, just like he is- was- when he's thinking about something.

And Cameron is our youngest. He's full of spirit and energy. I know he loves me, but it's his father that he craves attention from. I love to see them together playing ball in the backyard or working on a puzzle or doing a board game in the living room. He misses his father very much…"

Catherine's chin quivered as she fought back tears, and her voice cracked. "…And the most difficult thing I ever had to tell him was that his Daddy was never coming back. That's the hardest thing for a child to hear and so hard for a mother to say."

"Mrs. Khury, do you know how your husband died?"

"No. They say he killed himself. But that's impossible. Ahmed loved life. He loved me, his children. He loved his life with us."

"Did he ever talk about suicide?"

"Never."

"Did he ever appear to be depressed?"

"No, never. Just the ups and downs that we all have in life."

Brent guided Catherine through every detail of her courtship with Ahmed, their marriage, Ahmed's love for America and the day he received his citizenship. She even presented his citizenship certificate. The portrait of Ahmed as a true flag waving immigrant patriot was painted in red, white, and blue.

"How did Ahmed feel about his country?"

"Objection," said Nagel, "Calls for speculation."

"Overruled."

"Ahmed's country was the United States. He always talked about how much he loved America. Ahmed was so proud when he got his citizenship."

Catherine told the jury of their decision to have children, presented the family in photo albums from their births to their father's funeral; the story of a normal American family.

Next, Ahmed's professional life was presented. His work as an accountant for a reputable accounting firm, their financial statements; his promotions and prospects were all described, which would lead to the testimony of an actuary, who put a number on not only Ahmed's life expectancy if his life had not been cut short, but also what Catherine and the family could have hoped to gain from Ahmed's gainful employment as an accountant and retiree until that last of his expected years to live.

Brent then took Catherine through her and Ahmed's financial plan, their goals and desires, and Ahmed's generally good health before Guantanamo. Then he attacked the Patriot Act.

"Mrs. Khury, did you know that your house had been searched?"

"I didn't know it was the FBI. At first, I thought we had been robbed."

"What did you notice that was missing?"

"Our computers, and some of our most precious family photographs."

"Mrs. Khury, how did you feel when you found out that strangers had entered into your house and searched every part of it?"

"I felt violated. Like I had been raped."

"Mrs. Khury, you understand that you are asking the jury to award you damages for your loss, don't you?"

"Yes," she said, trembling.

"What amount of money are you claiming for the death of your husband?"

The tears streamed down Catherine's face like the first drops of rain in a summer storm.

"There is no amount of money that could ever compensate for the loss of my husband. I cannot put a price on him. His death has left my family lost, destroyed."

"Mrs. Khury, is there anything positive that could come from Ahmed's death?"

"If people can learn from it, maybe this will never happen to another innocent person." Nagel did not dare object this time, but he was biting his lip. "The ancestors of all American

223

people are immigrants like Ahmed. They are a compassionate people and they would never agree to what happened to Ahmed. His death was the martyrdom of a true patriot."

***

The last thing that Nagel wanted to appear to be was heartless and he limited his cross-examination accordingly.

"Mrs. Khury, I'm sorry to have to put you through cross-examination on such a sensitive issue, but you understand that I must, don't you?"

"Yes, I do."

"Mrs. Khury, you did not see Ahmed die, did you?"

"No."

"And you hadn't talked to him for over eleven months at the time that he died, isn't that true?"

"They wouldn't let me!"

"Move to strike as non-responsive, Your Honor."

"Granted.   The jury will disregard the answer.   Mrs. Khury, please just answer the question."

"I'm sorry, Your Honor."

"It is true, that you didn't talk to him, isn't it?"

"Yes."

"So, if he was depressed, you wouldn't have known it, isn't that true?"

"He didn't kill himself!"

"Move to strike as non-responsive, Your Honor."

"Granted.   Mrs. Khury, we know this is difficult to talk about, but you must only answer from your own personal knowledge.   The jury will disregard the answer."

"You wouldn't have known anything about his state of mind because you didn't speak with him, isn't that correct?"

"Yes, but Ahmed was a strong man."

"Isn't it true, though, Mrs. Khury, that you don't know what was going through your husband's mind right before he died?"

"Yes that is true, Mr. Nagel. I didn't. I cannot imagine what could have been going through his mind in that horrible place."

Nagel took Catherine through an examination of Ahmed's family.

"Mrs. Khury, you had never met Ahmed's brother Sabeen, had you?"

"No."

"So you didn't know anything about his activities in Iraq, isn't that correct?"

"I know he was a grocer."

"Objection, Your Honor, hearsay."

"Sustained. The jury will disregard the answer."

"And you didn't know about his ties to al Qaeda, did you?"

"Objection," said Brent. "Calls for speculation."

"Sustained."

Brent was satisfied with Catherine's testimony. It looked like it had touched the jury, and nothing that Nagel did on cross-examination could change those emotions. Brent decided not to put Catherine back on re-direct. At break, he put his arm around her and led her out of the courtroom, where she immediately poured herself into the nearest bench and cried.

CHAPTER THIRTY-SIX

It was dark when Brent pulled into his driveway. Just enough time to feed the cat and himself, go over his notes for the next day and sleep a few hours. When he opened the door he practically fell over the cat who had heard his car pull up and was waiting impatiently for her dinner. She protested vehemently.

"Okay, okay, I'm sorry."

Calico bounded off for the kitchen. Then the phone rang. Brent wasn't much of a phone person, and when it rang, it always annoyed him, especially after a day like today. It was Debbie.

"How did it go today?"

"Fine, first day of trial."

"Wanna come over?"

"Deb, I can't. I've got trial tomorrow."

"What, you're like a boxer or a hockey player or something? No sex before the big game?"

"Who said anything about sex?"

"I think I just did. Change your mind?"

Brent laughed, and looked down at Calico, who was angrily swishing her tail like she was swatting at a fly. "Can I bring my cat?"

"Honey, you can bring whatever you want."

"Okay, I'll be over a little later, but I can't stay long."

No sooner had he hung up the phone, but it rang again.

"Dude!" It was Rick.

"What's up? Have any leads on the four thugs turned up?"

"No, I just called to see if you wanted to grab a beer."

"Sorry dude, I just had a better offer."

"Better than me? I doubt that."

"I'm sure you can't do what I was offered. Maybe you can, but it would gross me out."

"Debbie Does Dallas?"

"Right."

"Go over there, fuck her and then join me at Sonny's."

"Now I know why you never got married."

"We've got trial prep."

"I've got real trial prep."

"So I just heard. Well, I'm sure your client will benefit from a happy lawyer tomorrow."

"Goodbye, Rick." Brent hung up the phone as the cat threatened to claw her way up his leg. He poured out a generous portion of dry food and she just sat there, looking at it.

"What? Are you kidding me?" Brent got a can of cat food, opened it, and mixed some of it with the dry kibble.

"Now are you happy?"

The cat sniffed at the mixture, hesitated, and looked up at Brent, who walked away.

***

Brent opened his eyes. He couldn't see anything. It was deadly silent. He tried to move, but was unable to move his arms or legs. He strained to breathe against the hood that threatened to suffocate him, and blocked out all sensation. All he could feel was his naked body against a cold concrete floor. He screamed, but could not even hear himself scream. In his panic, he bucked against his restraints, and felt the cold steel burning into his wrists. Suddenly, he could hear someone calling him from far away. It was a faint sound.

"Brent?" Brent rustled, and his startled eyes opened in terror. He felt tingling on his sweaty neck.

"Brent, are you okay?" It was Debbie.

"Yeah, I'm fine. Must have had a nightmare."

Debbie stroked his back to calm him down. "Go back to sleep."

"Can't, big day tomorrow. Sorry Deb, I have to go."

***

Brent got home about midnight, just long enough to take a shower, review his outline for the next day, and get to bed. It was all about getting the evidence in. The visit to Debbie's took an edge off the adrenaline cocktail he had been working on all day. *Hopefully there will be no more nightmares,* he thought.

He lay in bed, going over his notes, until he found himself reading the same line over and over again.

Then the alarm went off.

CHAPTER THIRTY-SEVEN

"The Plaintiff calls Sergeant William Brown as an adverse witness."

"Sergeant Brown, please step forward and be sworn."

Scrgeant Brown took a seat in the witness box, which seemed to be too small for him. Under cross-examination, Brown outlined Ahmed's "processing" during his first six weeks at Guantanamo, as he did in his deposition, as if such things were completely normal, and only left out little things like waterboarding, dry-boarding, beatings, and mock executions.

Brent didn't expect to crack Brown, like Masters Mason, and get him to admit that Ahmed had died in the feeding room, and that he and Nurse Benson had covered it all up. But he tried his best to elicit any details that could be exploited by the testimony of others, or used in his argument.   Presenting a trial was like working a huge jigsaw puzzle for the jury, where half of the pieces were missing.   Unfortunately, what really happened would never be known.

"Sergeant Brown, when Mr. Khury was brought to Camp 7, he was chained, hooded so he could not see, his ears muffed so he could not hear, and his hands muffed so he could not feel, isn't that correct?"

"Mr. Khury was delivered by the Air Force wearing their standard issue equipment to ensure the safety of their personnel and the integrity of Camp 7, whose location is classified."

"Move to strike as non-responsive, Your Honor."

"Granted.   Sergeant Brown, you must answer the question."

"I will rephrase it, Your Honor."

Sergeant Brown looked down at the one hooded and shackled detainee that had just arrived. He was sitting in the dirt on his knees, naked, his hands shackled behind his back, his head waving from side to side, starving for any input to tell him where he was.

"Only one Haji?"

"Yes, Sergeant," said the Corporal. "This one has been tagged as a high profile non-privileged combatant, sir."

"He looks like Stevie-fuckin' Wonder movin' that fuckin' head round like that."

The Corporal laughed.

"Let him sit here for a few hours. Then get him washed, searched and beard and head shaved. Do the standard cavity search. Make sure he's not hiding anything up his ass."

"Yes, Sergeant. Then what?"

"Then what Corporal? What do I do with shit I scrape off the bottom of my shoe?"

"I don't know, Sergeant."

"Throw him in the hole, Corporal."

"Yes, Sergeant."

"Mr. Khury was issued a basic comforts-only package, which consisted of an ISO mat, one blanket, one towel, one roll of toilet paper, toothpaste and a finger toothbrush, one Styrofoam cup, one bar of soap, a copy of the camp rules, and a Koran."

"What about a jumpsuit, and a basic comforts package?"

"Corporal, did you hear what I just said?"

"Yes, Sergeant."

"Good, because I was thinking for a minute that you'd gone deaf, or, worse yet, that I'd gone dumb."

"No Sergeant."

"Throw this fuckin' Haji in the hole with nothing. Is that clear, Corporal?"

"Yes, Sergeant."

"Phase Two of Behavior Management was a program to isolate Mr. Khury and foster his dependence on the interrogator," Brown testified.

"How was that supposed to be done?"

"By exploiting his sense of disorientation and disorganization."

Sergeant Brown looked at Ahmed, hanging lifelessly from the pole after the mock execution.

"Looks like this Haji has pissed his pants."

"Yes, Sergeant," said the young private with the M16.

"We've gotta teach these Arabs not to piss in their pants. We're not a laundry service, are we, Private?"

238

"No, Sergeant."

"Save the jumpsuit for him for later. He won't need it now. Take him back and throw him in the hole. Lights out."

"Yes, Sergeant."

"Mr. Khury was treated in the spirit of the Geneva Conventions," Brown continued in his testimony.

"But as a non-privileged enemy combatant, you were trained that the Geneva Conventions did not apply to him, isn't that correct?"

"Yes, sir."

"And that was according to your standard operating procedure, is that correct?"

"Yes, sir."

"Were dogs used in Phase Two?"

"Yes, sir."

"Large German Shepherd dogs, like police dogs, isn't that correct?"

"Yes, sir."

"You used them for management, correct?"

"Yes, sir."

"For example, when you moved Mr. Khury around the camp, you brought the dog into his cell, correct?"

"Yes, sir."

"And then you placed wrist cuffs and ankle cuffs on Mr. Khury, is that correct?"

"Yes, sir."

"And then you placed the hood over his head, correct?"

"Sometimes, when needed."

"Is that a yes?"

"Yes, sir."

"And ear muffs, so he could not hear."

"Yes, sir."

"Yet you still considered him to be a threat, after all those precautions."

"Yes, sir."

"So you still needed the dog to escort him, correct?"

"Yes, sir, for the safety of extraction personnel."

The team of MPs, dressed in riot gear, with a large un-muzzled German shepherd in tow, entered Ahmed's cell, casting light into the darkness. They let the dog loose and he ran at Ahmed, growling.

"Don't move Haji!" commanded one of the soldiers.

The dog stood a few feet in front of Ahmed, barking. Ahmed recoiled in fear, whereupon the dog, sensing movement, charged at Ahmed, burying his nose in Ahmed's crotch, growling.

"I said don't move. If you move, he'll take your balls off."

"Mr. Khury was kept in isolation for six weeks, is that correct?" asked Brent.

"Yes, sir."

"And that is standard operating procedure?"

"Yes, sir."

"You didn't consider that torture?"

"We don't torture detainees, sir."

"Move to strike as non-responsive."

"Granted. Answer the question," Judge Henley said.

"You don't consider isolation to be torture?"

"No, sir."

"During those six weeks, you used sensory deprivation on Mr. Khury, is that correct?"

"Yes, sir."

"Again, that was standard operating procedure?"

"Yes, sir."

"And you don't consider that torture?"

"We are not allowed to torture detainees at Camp 7, sir."

"Move to strike as non-responsive."

"Granted. The witness will answer the question."

"Yes or no, Sergeant, do you consider it to be torture?"

"No, sir."

CHAPTER THIRTY-EIGHT

Brent continued the grueling cross-examination of Sergeant Brown as an adverse witness. The Sergeant was not going to break. He had been through more stressful situations than this cross examination in his tours in Afghanistan and Iraq. If he was lying, and Brent was sure he was, it wasn't going to come out on cross. Brent had to zero in on items that he knew the Sergeant would admit, fully aware of the fact that the real truth would never be exposed.

"Was Mr. Khury kept in stress positions during Phase Two?"

"Yes, sir."

"When was he kept in stress positions?"

"Before interrogation by the JIG."

"In fact, Mr. Khury was forced to stand, with his hands cuffed to a chain in the ceiling of his cell, for eight hours at a time, isn't that correct?'

"It depends."

"Move to strike as non-responsive."

"Granted, the witness will answer the question."

"Sometimes."

"And, other times, he was forced to fit himself into a steel box on the floor, or stand on one leg with both of his arms up for 30 minutes, isn't that correct?"

"Sometimes."

"Again, this was standard operating procedure, isn't that correct?"

"Yes, sir."

"Get into the box, Ahab," said Sergeant Brown, surrounded by four men in riot gear.

"I can't fit in that box, Sergeant Brown." Ahmed looked at the small steel box on the floor.

"Company!"

One of the men sprayed pepper spray in Ahmed's eyes. He recoiled in pain, tears running down his face.

"Okay, I will try."

"Don't try, do!"

"And you didn't consider this stress position to be torture?" asked Brent.

"No, sir."

"This standard operating procedure, is that set forth in a manual for the operation of Camp 7?"

"Yes, sir."

"Showing you a document that has been marked for identification as Exhibit 23, can you identify this document as the manual of standard operating procedures for Camp 7?" Brown flipped through the exhibit.

"Yes, sir, it looks like it, sir."

"Sergeant Brown, after six weeks, was Mr. Khury moved out of isolation?"

"Yes, sir."

"And he was placed in the general population?"

"Yes, sir."

"Showing you a series of photos marked as Exhibits 24 through 30, do these photos accurately depict the corridor outside Mr. Khury's cell and the cell itself?"

"They appear to, sir."

Ahmed was instructed to put on an orange jump suit, then he was hooded, and moved. He could hear the sound of loud rock music in the distance. His escorts, dressed in riot gear, with dark visors and earplugs, opened the steel door to the cellblock. As they did, the sound of AC/DC blaring and reverberating against the concrete walls felt like a second steel door to pass through. They opened the door to Ahmed's new cell, pushed him in, and ripped his hood off to a blinding light, as intense as the sun.

"Welcome to your new home," said one of the team, a private with buck teeth, and slammed the door.

The music and light show continued 24/7. Ahmed tried to put his hands over his ears, but he couldn't because they were still handcuffed. He closed his eyes, and wished for the isolation and darkness that had been his enemy for so many weeks.

"Was overstimulation used on Mr. Khury while he was in this stage of behavior modification?" Brent asked.

"Yes, sir."

"When you say over stimulation, do you mean that Mr. Khury's cell was bombarded with loud rock music for long periods of time?"

"Yes, sir."

"And intense bright lights?"

"Yes, sir."

"And you do not consider this torture?"

"No, sir."

"And this is standard operating procedure?"

"Yes, sir."

"Isn't it true, Sergeant Brown, that you were trained by your command in the definition of torture?"

"Yes, sir."

"And this definition of torture that you learned in your training is, 'That which inflicts serious pain, likely to be experienced by great bodily injury, such as the destruction of an organ?'"

"Yes, sir."

"Do you know what waterboarding is, Sergeant?"

"Yes, sir."

"That is where a person is immobilized on a flat surface, and water is poured over their face to simulate drowning, is that correct?"

"Yes, sir."

"And you contend that Mr. Khury was never waterboarded?"

"Correct, sir."

"Even the secretary of defense doesn't think that waterboarding is torture, isn't that correct Sergeant?"

"Objection! Calls for speculation!" Nagel said, sharply.

"Sustained."

"Do you know what dry-boarding is?"

"Yes, sir."

"That is a process of sticking cloths in a person's mouth, then taping their nose and mouth shut, is that correct?"

"Yes, sir."

"And it is your contention that Mr. Khury was never dry-boarded?"

"That is correct, sir."

"Sergeant Brown, were you called by Corporal Reeding during the last force-feeding of Mr. Khury?"

"Yes, sir."

"Did Corporal Reeding express to you that there was an emergency?"

"Yes, sir."

"But you don't think there was an emergency, do you Sergeant?"

"No, sir. The detainee coughed up his feeding tube. It happens all the time."

"Yet this was the last time he was force-fed, isn't that correct?"

"Yes, sir."

"Because the next day, he was found dead in his cell, isn't that correct?"

"Yes, sir."

"Immediately after that feeding, Sergeant, you put Mr. Khury in his cell, is that correct?"

"Yes, sir."

"You and Nurse Benson, is that correct?"

"Yes, sir."

"Isn't it standard operating procedure for the feeding team to take the detainee back to his cell?"

"Yes, sir."

"So you broke procedure?"

"Yes, sir."

"And you broke procedure because the situation called for different handling, isn't that true?"

"Yes, sir."

"And again, Sergeant Brown, Mr. Khury was found hanging from the wire mesh ceiling in his cell, is that correct?"

"Yes, sir."

"A ceiling that is eight feet high?"

"Yes, sir."

"Nobody else saw you and Nurse Benson take Mr. Khury back to his cell, correct?"

"That is correct, sir."

Brent was at a crossroads. He knew that Brown would never admit what really happened, but he needed a thread of the truth to come out. For that, Brown needed to be agitated, off his game. Whether he slipped or not, it didn't matter. The jury would hear where Brent was going and would draw their own conclusions.

"And isn't it also correct, Sergeant Brown that Mr. Khury was dead when you brought him back to his cell?"

"No, sir!" said Brown, raising his voice.

"You don't have to scream Sergeant, we can hear you."

"Objection, argumentative," barked Nagel.

"Sustained."

Isn't it true that, after you took Mr. Khury's lifeless body to his cell, you strung him up with a regular orange jumpsuit to make it look like he had hanged himself?"

"That is not true, sir. I did no such thing!"

"Showing you what has been marked as Exhibit 31, Sergeant, is this the jumpsuit that Mr. Khury was found dead in?" Brown glanced at the tag, and then averted his eyes.

"It appears to be, sir."

"Would it surprise you, Sergeant that this jumpsuit is not one that cannot be tied or torn?"

"No, sir."

"Mr. Khury had talked about suicide, isn't that correct?"

"Yes, sir."

"And every detainee who was suicidal was given a special jumpsuit that could not be torn or tied into a noose, isn't that correct?"

"Yes, sir."

"Your honor, I submit as Exhibit 32, a report by the United States Navy Investigative Criminal Investigation Service, and I quote, "the detainee's jumpsuit was tested and identified as a standard issue orange jumpsuit. Move to admit Exhibit 32 into evidence, Your Honor.

"No objection? It is received."

"In fact, that was standard operating procedure in the case of a suicide threat to give every suicidal detainee a special jumpsuit, isn't that correct Sergeant?"

"Yes, sir. But Khury was not considered a suicide threat."

"No further questions at this time, Your Honor."

CHAPTER THIRTY-NINE

In order to rehabilitate Brown and lessen the negative blow of his testimony, Nagel took him through his duties at Gitmo, their humane treatment of detainees, the anti-torture policy (under their definition of torture), and his contacts with Ahmed.

"Did Mr. Khury ever express a desire to kill himself?"

"Yes, sir."

"How many times?"

"Several times, sir."

"And yet he was never placed on suicide watch, isn't that correct?"

"No, sir. He was evaluated and found not to be suicidal."

"Evaluated by whom?"

"The Naval psychiatrist, sir."

"So, you took the precaution of having him evaluated, yet he still hung himself?"

"Objection! Assumes facts not in evidence."

"Sustained. The jury will disregard the question. Mr. Nagel, please continue."

"Sergeant Brown, after his suicide evaluation, did you, nevertheless, take any precautions to guarantee Mr. Khury's safety?"

"Yes, sir."

"What precautions?"

"The guards looked inside his cell approximately every one to three minutes to make sure he was okay."

"And how long did this procedure continue?"

"Until he was found dead, sir."

***

Corporal Brian Reeding took the stand, in his crisp dress uniform, looking very cool and collected. He was Brent's best adverse witness, and Brent was counting on him filling in the blanks for the jury that had been left hanging from Sergeant Brown's testimony. Brent took Reeding through a series of questions establishing his role at Guantanamo, and his position as head of the feeding team.

"Corporal Reeding, you made an emergency call to Sergeant Brown during Mr. Khury's last feeding, is that correct?"

"Yes, sir. I was new on the job and panicked when he coughed up his feeding tube."

Brent felt like he had been hit right between the eyes with a hammer. Reeding had changed his testimony, but not so much so that it conflicted with his deposition testimony.

"Corporal Reeding, you understand that you are under oath, don't you?"

"Yes, sir."

"And that oath is just as serious and binding upon you as the oath you took when you joined the Army, do you understand that?"

"Yes, sir."

"Corporal, you testified in your deposition that you called Sergeant Brown because Mr. Khury was complaining that the feeding tube was hurting him and he subsequently coughed up the tube, is that correct?"

"Yes, sir."

"And you thought that he may be in danger, correct?"

"Yes, sir, but I was wrong."

"Move to strike after 'yes, sir.'"

"Denied."

"When you called Sergeant Brown, he cleared the room, is that correct?"

"Yes, sir."

"By clearing the room, he instructed everyone but Nurse Benson to leave, correct?"

"Yes, sir."

"Corporal, you thought Mr. Khury was in serious danger, isn't that correct?"

"I guess I overreacted."

"Move to strike as non-responsive."

"Motion granted. The witness will answer the question." Corporal Reeding looked lost in thought.

"I can't breathe! It's in wrong!"

Ahmed choked. He couldn't speak anymore. He began to cough incessantly, then spit up vomit and blood.

"Stop the procedure!" Corporal Reeding whipped out his radio and called Sergeant Brown.

"Sergeant, you'd better get down here, we've got a situation! What the fuck, man, he's not breathing! You're a nurse, do something!"

Nurse Benson looked confused and disoriented. He was in a panic. Ahmed's head had fallen to his lap, and there was blood, vomit and Ensure coming trickling out of his mouth. Benson checked his pulse.

"There's no pulse!"

"Do something, man!"

Benson tried to revive Ahmed. He and Reeding removed the restraints and set Ahmed on the floor. Benson gave him CPR. Each time he gave Ahmed mouth to mouth, more fluid came out, but it was no use. Ahmed was lifeless.

Sergeant Brown ran in. "Clear the room!" he ordered.

"Corporal Reeding?" inquired Brent, and Reeding seemed to snap back into consciousness.

"Yes, sir?"

"When Sergeant Brown cleared the room, he, Nurse Benson, and Mr. Khury were the only ones left in the room, is that correct?" asked Brent.

"Yes, sir."

"Corporal, do you remember when you and I met in Miami?" Reeding looked like something had just hit him in the head.

"I can't answer that question."

"Your honor?" Brent implored.

"Objection, argumentative!" urged Nagel.

"Counsel, approach the bench please."

Nagel, his second chair and Brent approached the bench.

"Mr. Marks, what is going on here?"

"He's not being consistent with his prior statements, Your Honor," said Brent.

"Well, you have his deposition transcript. Read it into the record."

"I object to this line of questioning, Your Honor, it's too prejudicial for the jury," said Nagel.

"What's your offer of proof, Mr. Marks?"

"I interviewed the witness in Miami, at his request, Your Honor, and his version of the story was very different than the one he's telling today."

"I'll allow it. The witness cannot choose if he wants to answer a question or not. We're going to break for lunch. I want you to consult with the defense, disclose everything that was said in the interview, and when the break is over, we go again, understood?"

***

At the break, Reeding joined Nagel at the counsel table. The entire gallery had dispersed, except for one young man in the far right corner. Brent made eye contact with him and the guy got up and left.

"Rick, somebody got to this guy. You've gotta find out what happened. He's our best witness."

"Dude, you've got to pull a Benedict Arnold on him."

"I know."

"I'll see what I can find out."

"And while you're at it, there's this strange young dude that comes in every day, like this case is some kind of a class project for him or something. He always sits in the back. Check him out too, okay?"

"Yeah, sure. I know which one you mean." Rick left the courtroom.

***

As Rick walked out, he recognized the young guy sitting on bench in the corridor. He looked about 25, and had a military-style crew cut. Rick caught his eye as he approached, and the guy averted his glance. Just as it seemed he would pass him, Rick took a seat next to him on the bench and started going over his notes. He looked up from them and smiled, and the guy forced a nervous smile in return.

"Do I know you?" Rick asked.

"Me? No sir, no, we've never met," said the guy, squirming in his seat. He spoke in a Southern accent.

"You look familiar," said Rick, messing with the guy's brain. The guy glanced away and fidgeted.

"Don't know why you'd say that."

"Interesting case, huh?"

"Yes, sir, I guess."

"What's your connection to it?"

"Me? Nothing, sir."

"Then what are you doing here?"

"Just thought it would be fun to watch."

"Rick Penn," said Rick, holding out his hand.

"Joshua Anderson. It's nice to meet you, sir."

"Relax, dude, nobody calls me sir."

"Force of habit, I guess."

"Military?"

"United States Marine Corps." The guy had wild eyes, and Rick really did have a funny feeling that he had seen those eyes before, but he could not place it. Little did he know that he was face to face with Balls.

CHAPTER FORTY

Rick came up with a big nothing in checking on Corporal Reeding, but there wasn't much time during the lunch break to do any real investigating. However, Rick shared Brent's hunch that someone had threatened or coerced Reeding into changing his story. Having no concrete facts, Brent had to fly by the seat of his pants.

"Isn't it true, Corporal Reeding, that you have become more and more definite in your belief that you overreacted in the feeding room as time goes on?"

"I don't understand the question."

"Isn't it true that, during your deposition, I asked you the same questions, and you did not tell me that you overreacted?"

"Yes, sir."

"Isn't it true that your first impression after the incident was that Mr. Khury was in trouble?"

"Yes, sir."

"And as time has gone forward, you've thought about it many times, haven't you?"

"Yes, sir."

"And how you think about it now is different than your first impression, isn't it?"

"I suppose so, sir."

"Who else did you discuss the case with after your deposition?"

"Sir?"

"Who did you discuss the incident with?"

"Mr. Nagel."

"Who else?"

"My CO."

"That's Colonel Masters?"

"Yes."

"What did you discuss with him?"

"I don't recall sir."

"But you do recall discussing it with me, isn't that true, Corporal?"

264

"Yes, sir.   And you promised me anonymity."

Brent didn't want to move to strike everything after 'yes, sir,' even though he knew it would be granted. He didn't want the jury to think he was trying to hide anything.

"Since you've talked to Mr. Nagel, you know I was not bound by that promise, don't you?"

"Yes, sir."

"You told me that you were concerned that things had gone too far at Gitmo, didn't you?"

"Yes, sir."

"You told me that you thought they were waterboarding in interrogations?"

"I don't know if they were, I just heard it…"

"Objection, hearsay!" snapped Nagel.

"Sustained.   The jury will disregard the answer. *Too late, they've already heard it.*

"And you thought they were dry-boarding, isn't that correct?"

"Objection, hearsay!"

265

"Sustained. The jury will disregard the answer. Counsel, please approach the bench." The judge was getting pissed, and for just reason.

"Mr. Marks, I let you have free rein, but I am not going to have a mistrial in this case."

"I'm sorry, Your Honor."

"Please wrap this one up."

Brent moved back to the counsel table, and then moved in for the kill. He had made a tactical decision. The jury could either believe that he was trying to manipulate the witness, or the witness was hiding something. He took the plunge.

"Before Mr. Khury's last feeding, you had seen detainees cough up feeding tubes, hadn't you?"

"Yes, sir."

"And you had heard them complain about the feeding tubes, didn't you?"

"Yes, sir."

"But this was different, wasn't it Corporal? You thought he was dead, didn't you?"

"I don't know."

"You did, you thought he was dead, isn't that true?"

"Objection, asked and answered."

"Sustained."

"You called Sergeant Brown because neither you nor Nurse Benson could revive him, isn't that correct?"

"I don't recall exactly, sir."

"Sure you do, Corporal, you've been in action on the battlefield, haven't you?"

"Yes, sir."

"And you've seen someone dead before, haven't you?"

"Yes, sir."

"And when you saw Ahmed Khury, slumped over in the feeding chair, with vomit and liquid and blood coming out of his mouth, you thought he was dead, didn't you?"

"I wasn't sure if he was alright or not."

"Move to strike as non-responsive."

"Denied." Brent had taken his shot, but it didn't pay off. Time to move on.

"Thank you, Your Honor. No further questions."

CHAPTER FORTY-ONE

After a short break, it was Nagel's turn to cross-examine Reeding, but he handed over the job to Joe Cicatto, his second chair.

"Corporal Reeding, do you think you overreacted to the incident in the feeding room with Mr. Khury?"

"Yes, sir, I did."

"Corporal, you testified that this was a new detail for you, is that correct?"

"Yes, sir."

"What kind of a medical background do you have, Corporal?"

"None, sir."

"No education in health care at all?"

"No, sir."

"So when you thought Mr. Khury was in danger when you observed him coughing up the feeding tube, you didn't really know if he was, isn't that correct?"

"Yes, sir."

"And you're not qualified to make an opinion as to the state of his health at the time, are you?"

"No, sir."

"And how long have you worked under the supervision of Sergeant Brown?"

"Almost a year now, sir. The entire length of my tour at Gitmo."

"Sergeant Brown runs a tight ship, doesn't he, Corporal?"

"Yes, sir, he does. He likes order."

"So, upon his arrival, when he asked you to clear the room, did that surprise you?"

"No, sir, not at all."

"It didn't surprise you that he took Mr. Khury back to his cell because you were hysterical, isn't that correct Corporal?"

"Yes, sir."

"You had several occasions to speak with Mr. Khury during his detention, didn't you?"

"Yes, sir, I did."

"How many times did Mr. Khury tell you he wanted to die?"

"Several times, sir."

"Upon hearing that from Mr. Khury, what, if anything, did you do?"

"I reported it to Sergeant Brown, and I recommended a psychiatric evaluation."

"As a result, did Mr. Khury receive a psychiatric evaluation?"

"Yes, he did."

***

Brent brought forth a multitude of guards, both male and female, who testified unemotionally and unaffectedly about the treatment that they had collectively inflicted on Ahmed.

Prolonged solitary confinement, sensory deprivation, and overstimulation were all terms that each knew well and each knew the purposes of the techniques. They testified how Ahmed was removed from his cell by teams of guards dressed in riot gear and flak jackets, and how he was routinely pepper-sprayed to subdue him so he could be thrown onto the floor and handcuffed. Several guards admitted that they had seen others "walling" him while hooded, as they were taking him in and out of his cell.

CHAPTER FORTY-TWO

James Benson, the naval nurse, continued the uniformed procession of witnesses, which was beginning to look like a military parade. As he took the witness stand, one would have thought it was the most uncomfortable seat in the world, and, for Benson, it probably was.

"Nurse Benson, how old are you?"

"I'm 25 years old, sir."

"Nurse Benson, you are a licensed practical nurse, is that correct?"

"Yes, sir."

"And you hold a certificate as such from the North Carolina Board of Nursing?"

"Yes, sir."

"How long have you held that certificate?"

"Approximately two years, sir."

"And did you receive training in enteral feeding?"

"Yes, sir."

"Where?"

"Camp Lejeune, North Carolina, sir."

"How long did that training program last?"

"Three days, sir."

"So this was a relatively new procedure for you when you fed Mr. Khury, isn't that correct?"

Benson coughed, and poured himself some water. "Excuse me," he said, and drank a sip. "Yes, sir."

"And you were the nurse who last fed Mr. Khury before his death, is that correct?"

"Yes, sir."

Brent took Benson through the feeding procedure, as he did in the deposition.

"Nurse Benson, I'm going to play a video for you of a feeding of Mr. Khury that has been marked for identification as Exhibit 36, and ask you if you can identify that the proper enteral feeding procedure is being used. Your honor, this video was obtained during discovery and is part of the official record."

"Proceed."

The old cliché that picture is worth a thousand words had obviously been coined before video was invented because video imparted a million words. As Brent observed the jury, he could see that every sickening detail of Ahmed's force-feeding had crept under their respective skins, and was crawling there and festering, like a boil.

"Nurse Benson, does this video properly depict the procedure of an enteral feeding?"

"Yes, sir, it does."

"And this procedure is performed at Guantanamo Bay Detention Camps without anesthesia, is that correct?"

"Well, we lubricate the end of the feeding tube with lidocaine, if the patient requests it."

"You sometimes lubricate the end of the tube with olive oil, is that correct?"

"Yes, sir. Detainees are given a choice between lidocaine and olive oil."

"And olive oil is an acceptable form of lubricant in the enteral feeding procedure?"

"Yes, sir."

"That is standard operating procedure, correct, to use either lidocaine or olive oil?"

"Yes, sir."

"Both are approved by your command?"

"Yes, sir."

"And showing you what has been marked for identification as Exhibit 37, can you identify this as an enteral feeding tube?"

"It looks like it, yes."

"This tube is a little over two feet long, wouldn't you say?"

"Yes, sir."

"And it all has to go in?"

"Yes, sir."

Next, Brent had to lay the foundation for Dr. Orozco's testimony, which ran the risk of losing the jury, due to the technical medical details. Brent put a chart on the easel and began to play "Bill Nye the Science Guy."

"Nurse Benson, does the chart I am showing you, which has been marked as Exhibit 38, depict a simple diagram of the human digestive system?"

"It appears to, yes sir."

"Now, in an enteral feeding, you would lubricate the end of the feeding tube, pass it through the nasal passages, through the esophagus, through the stomach, to the duodenum, the beginning of the small intestine, is that correct?" Brent asked, as he moved the pointer through the places in the diagram he was describing.

"Yes, sir."

"To do this, you have to pass this area, the upper esophageal sphincter, is that correct?"

"Yes, sir."

"Is that what gives the un-anaesthetized patient the choking sensation?"

"Yes, sir."

"It is the sphincter that keeps food from entering the trachea, or breathing tube, is that correct?"

"Yes, sir."

"Nurse Benson, do you know what aspiration is?"

Benson was building up a sweat, as if he was running a marathon. It was running from his hairline down his forehead and cheeks.

"Yes, sir."

"Have you ever seen a patient aspirate fluid during an enteral feeding procedure?"

"Yes, sir."

"Aspiration is a common complication during enteral feeding, is it not?"

"Yes, sir, it is."

"Do you have any monitoring devices in place for enteral feedings at Guantanamo Bay that show whether the feeding tube is properly positioned?"

Benson pulled at his collar, as if it was choking him. "No, sir."

"Nurse Benson, how many times had you performed the enteral feeding procedure on Mr. Khury?"

"About ten times."

"And at every feeding, Corporal Reeding was present, isn't that correct?"

"Yes, sir."

"And Mr. Khury gagged every time the tube was inserted, isn't that correct?"

"Yes, sir." A drop of sweat hit Benson's eye. He blinked from the sting of it and wiped his brow.

"Isn't it also correct that you and Corporal Reeding had already seen Mr. Khury cough up his feeding tube before the last feeding?"

"Yes, sir."

"More than once?"

"Yes, sir."

"Nurse Benson, during the last feeding, when Corporal Reeding yelled at you to stop the procedure, did you worry that the feeding tube may have been malpositioned?"

"Yes, sir."

"And did you stop the procedure?"

"Yes, sir."

"And you removed the feeding tube?"

"Yes, sir."

"At that point, Mr. Khury was unconscious, wasn't he, Nurse Benson?"

Benson hesitated, and took a measured breath. "He didn't appear to be feeling well."

"Move to strike as non-responsive, Your Honor."

"Granted."

"He was unconscious, wasn't he?"

"N-no, sir," Benson stammered.

"When Sergeant Brown came in and cleared the room, you didn't see him at first, did you Nurse Benson?"

"No, sir, I was occupied with Mr. Khury."

"Trying to save his life, is that correct?"

"No, no, sir. He was alive," Benson stammered.

"You didn't give him CPR?"

"No, sir."

"You and Sergeant Brown took Mr. Khury by gurney back to his cell, is that correct?"

"Yes, sir."

"We have to move quickly, Benson!" said Brown, as they entered Ahmed's cell and closed the door.

"Take off his jumpsuit?"

"Why?"

"Because it's a special one, Benson. God damn it, don't you squids learn how to obey orders? Just do it, man!"

Brown ran out, slamming the door behind him. He returned in a couple of minutes with another jump suit. Tying the leg into a noose, he slipped it around Ahmed's limp neck and pulled tight.

"Okay Benson, climb up on the sink. You have to tie the other end to the ceiling."

Benson got up on the steel sink/toilet combination and tied the end of the sleeve of the jumpsuit to the wire mesh ceiling as Brown held up the body. Vomit dripped out of Ahmed's mouth and onto his chest.

"Don't fuck it up! Is it done?"

"I'm trying," said Benson.

"Pull hard on it. We want to make sure it doesn't break."

Benson pulled hard on the sleeve. "It's in."

Brown gently let go of the body, which swung back and forth slightly like a pendulum, Ahmed's lifeless feet dangling about six inches above the ground.

"This never happened, Benson."

281

CHAPTER FORTY-THREE

Timothy Nagel's task of rehabilitating Nurse Benson was a tough one. He couldn't make Benson appear any less nervous, but he could emphasize the weak points in Brent's case. After all, Brent had not established that there was anything wrong with Ahmed, other than he "didn't feel well during the feeding," which would be what the jury would expect after seeing the videotape. There were no facts elicited about Ahmed's death, or the cover up, as Brent had expected there would be, at least from Reeding.

"Nurse Benson, on the last enteral feeding of Mr. Khury, you followed the enteral feeding procedures to the letter, isn't that correct?"

"Yes, sir."

"And you had followed the same procedures with every feeding of every detainee, is that correct?"

"Yes, sir."

"It happened many times, didn't it, that a detainee would complain about discomfort?"

"Objection, irrelevant," Brent interjected.

"Overruled. You may answer."

"Yes, almost every time."

"And it also happened that detainees coughed up their feeding tubes from time to time?"

"Objection, relevance."

"Overruled."

"Yes, sir."

"So, was there anything unusual about this feeding with Mr. Khury, other than Corporal Reeding's overreaction?"

"Objection, lack of foundation, assumes facts not in evidence, argumentative."

"Sustained. The jury will disregard the question. Counsel, please rephrase."

"What was unusual, if anything, during the last feeding of Mr. Khury?"

"The way that Corporal Reeding reacted to Mr. Khury coughing up his feeding tube."

"Other than that, the feeding procedure was normal?"

"Yes, sir."

"It was also not unusual to take Mr. Khury back to his cell by gurney, was it?"

"No, sir."

"Why not?"

"When detainees experience discomfort, we always take them back to their cells by gurney."

"Thank you, Nurse Benson, I have no further questions."

CHAPTER FORTY-FOUR

Dr. Orozco waddled up to the stand, wiggled into the witness chair, faced the jury, and smiled. Despite his obesity, he had a pleasant manner about him and he made good eye contact with the members of the jury.

"Dr. Orozco, you are a medical examiner, is that correct?"

"Yes."

"Can you please summarize for the jury, your background, education and experience?"

"Certainly. I have over 30 years' experience as a pathologist and medical examiner. I hold an MD, a PhD, and a medical license in the state of California, where I am board certified in clinical, anatomic and forensic pathology. I also have a JD from Southwestern University School of Law and am a licensed attorney in California and New York. I am a Diplomate of the American Board of Pathology. I worked as a Chief Medical Examiner for the County of Los Angeles for ten years and another 10 years for the Federal Bureau of Investigation. I have testified as an expert witness in hundreds of trials."

"Could you just give us a brief description of what forensic pathology is?"

"I can. Pathology, the larger field, is one of the medical specialties, and it has basically two subcategories; anatomic pathology and clinical pathology. Anatomic pathology deals with the study of disease, that's really what the word means, from actual anatomic inspection. So it involves areas such as performing autopsies, looking at surgical specimens under a microscope, those sorts of things where there is an actual naked eye or microscopic examination for the most part.

"Clinical pathology is the laboratory area, and clinical pathologists usually head a hospital laboratory and serve as consultant to hospital physicians in ordering and interpretation of tests. Forensic pathology is a special area in pathology. The word "forensic" comes from the Latin word "forum", which was the Roman courtroom. The term is applied because forensic pathologists are often involved in clarifying medical or scientific questions that come up in the courtroom. Most forensic pathologists work in a coroner's office or medical examiner's office and investigate sudden or unexpected deaths."

"How many autopsies have you done in your career, doctor?"

"Too many to count. I would say many hundreds, maybe in the thousands."

To eliminate questions of bias, Brent asked Dr. Orozco to point out that he, like any medical expert, worked for money, what his hourly rate was, and the fact that he had worked on both criminal and civil cases, for both the plaintiff and the defendant.

"Dr. Orozco, please tell the jury what materials and reports you viewed in preparation for today's testimony."

"I reviewed the autopsy report of the Naval Criminal Investigation Service, the medical records of the decedent, Ahmed Khury, from his regular medical doctor, the medical records of the decedent from the Guantanamo Bay Detention Camp, my own report, which was based on my own autopsy of the decedent, and, of course, I listened to the testimony of all the witnesses up to this point."

Dr. Orozco was very comfortable with a jury. He had done this many times, and knew how to put the story to them in layman's terms. Brent identified all of the exhibits that Dr. Orozco had mentioned.

"Dr. Orozco, as a result of your review, and your examination of the body, do you have an opinion within a reasonable degree of medical certainty what caused Ahmed's death?

"Yes, I do."

"Would you please tell the jury your opinion?"

"As a result of my autopsy, which concurred with the NCIS autopsy report, there were traces of olive oil in his nostrils and lungs. The use of olive oil in enteral feeding is, in my opinion, gross negligent medical care in reckless disregard of standard medical practices."

"Why, Doctor?"

"Since olive oil is not water soluble, once this fatty type oil gets into the lungs, it can cause a serious disease called lipoid pneumonia. I ran a check on his pulmonary tissues and confirmed that he had this pathology."

"Was that the cause of Ahmed's death?"

"No. His lungs were weakened by the lipoid pneumonia, which made him more susceptible to further injury, but, in this case, the cause of Mr. Khury's death was aspiration of the liquid nutrients. This is supported by the findings of the nutrients in his lungs. He simply drowned due to an improper insertion of the feeding tube."

Brent put up some graphic photographs from Orozco's autopsy, and the doctor used them to illustrate his testimony further, using a pointer.

I also examined Mr. Khury's neck and head to eliminate asphyxiation by hanging as a cause of death. I found lack of ligature marks consistent with death by hanging. In other words, I found no abrasions or hemorrhages in the skin and indeed no hemorrhages in the eyes that one would expect to occur if he had been alive when he was hanged."

"Are you saying that Mr. Khury was hanged after he was already dead?"

"That's how it appears from the forensic evidence. When I do an autopsy, the body "talks" to me. It leaves physical signs, which communicate the cause of death. In this case, I examined the tissue around the ligature, and there was no traces of any reaction to the hanging that you would expect from a live subject."

"Doctor, do you have an opinion within a reasonable medical certainty what injuries Mr. Khury suffered as a result of his aspirating the liquid nutrients?"

"Yes. As I stated, Mr. Khury literally drowned from the presence of fluid in his lungs. This drowning occurred slowly, as he was able to speak and even cough while it was in process. Aside from the obvious pain that this procedure – done without anesthesia – caused before he aspirated the fluid, after the fluid had been completely assumed by the lungs, I would say that he suffered great pain for approximately 8 minutes before losing consciousness."

"Do you have an opinion within a reasonable degree of medical certainty as to whether the pain and suffering endured by Mr. Khury was a result of his aspirating the liquid nutrients?"

"Mr. Khury's pain and suffering was, in fact, from the enteral feeding procedure and aspirating the liquid nutrients."

"As a result of your examination and all of the evidence you observed doctor, do you have an opinion as to the standard of care exercised in this enteral feeding procedure?"

"Yes. It is my opinion that Mr. Khury's death was caused by gross negligent medical care in reckless disregard of standard medical practices by an improper insertion of the enteral feeding tube, and the failure to make adjustments to the position of the tube after he complained, which adjustments would have most certainly saved his life."

"No further questions, Your Honor."

"Cross?"

"Thank you, Your Honor," said Nagel.

"Dr. Orozco, you testified that the autopsy you performed on Mr. Khury was a second autopsy, correct?"

"Yes."

"And when you examined the body, the internal organs had already been dissected and examined, correct?"

"Yes, but there were tissue samples preserved in paraffin blocks."

"Nevertheless, there were limitations on the second autopsy, isn't that true?"

"Yes, but often a second autopsy looks at things that the pathologist in the first did not and it, along with the findings of the first autopsy, presents a more complete picture of the cause of death."

"Move to strike after "Yes," Your Honor."

"Granted. The jury will disregard everything after 'yes'."

"The stomach had been removed and dissected already, isn't that correct?"

"Yes."

"And the intestines were dissected already, correct?"

"That is correct."

"And the lungs had been dissected and examined already?"

"Yes."

"And body fluids that you would have liked to examine were already examined and removed, isn't that correct?"

"That is correct."

"So, Doctor, wouldn't you have been able to make a better evaluation of the cause of death if you had been the pathologist who performed the first autopsy?"

"Objection," interrupted Brent. "Calls for speculation."

"Overruled."

"I suppose so."

"Thank you, Doctor. No further questions, Your Honor."

"Nagel, pleased with himself, took his seat at the counsel table, his lips curling into a smile that Brent wanted to slap right off his face.

"Redirect?"

"Thank you, Your Honor." Brent stood up.

"Doctor Orozco, your opinion is not based solely on your autopsy, is it?"

"No, it is not."

"What else is it based on?"

"I based my opinion on the observations during the autopsy I performed, and the report of the autopsy performed by the NCIS pathologist."

"But you disagree with their conclusion?"

"Yes."

"Why?"

"Because of the traces of enteral feeding liquid in the lungs in the NCIS report as well as my examination, as well as the lack of physical evidence of death by asphyxiation."

"And this evidence was apparent from your examination of the body?"

"Absolutely."

CHAPTER FORTY-FIVE

Brent found Rick sitting at a corner table at Sonny's, in front of a heaping pile of some kind of Chinese style appetizer. When he walked in, Rick held up a mug of beer in a toasting motion and smiled. Brent was not in a smiling mood.

"So what did you find out?" Brent asked.

"It's good to see you too, buddy."

"Come on!"

"I've got a surprise for you."

"Tell me about Reeding first."

"Okay, but my surprise is better. It seems that after our meeting with Reeding in Miami he went out and got drunk, and, well, some other things, and as he was staggering out of the strip club-slash-whorehouse, he was paid a visit by some masked men."

"Like me."

"Yes, amazingly similar. Anyway, they beat the living crap out of him. Put him in the hospital."

"Let me guess, he didn't press charges?"

"You got that right."

"You have to find those guys, Rick."

"And make gold from mercury: Okay boss, no problem."

"Seriously, we need them and we need them now."

"Okay, I'm on it. Can I finish my Chinese 'whatever-the-fuck-this-is' first?"

"Of course. Now, what's the surprise?"

"Ah, I see curiosity has finally conquered the 'too serious' beast."

"Are you going to tell me?"

"First you have to guess what number I'm thinking of."

"Fuck, man, do you ever take anything seriously?"

"Not during happy hour I don't."

"Okay, give it up."

"What number?"

"What? Five."

Rick smirked like a gambler who had just won a bet.

"It's not five."

"Oh, it's five," Brent said, brandishing his fist. "Because if you don't tell me now I'm gonna plant these five knuckles right between your eyes."

"You're really no fun today. Alright, are you ready for this?"

Brent regarded Rick with childish impatience, like he had just swallowed a bug. Rick grinned through it.

"The good Colonel Masters had a very interesting tour of duty before his assignment to Gitmo. Remember the Abu Ghraib scandal?"

"Yeah. With the pictures of naked prisoners being tortured by soldiers."

"And the CIA. But there was a huge cover up and they just sent the sacrificial lambs to court-martial as fall guys. The stink rose all the way to the top."

"I know. Rumsfeld offered to resign over it."

"Turns out the torture was sanctioned by the Department of Justice."

"The memos from the DOJ telling the president's staff that torture was legal."

"Dude, it's not torture. It's *enhanced interrogation techniques*. One of the guys who wrote the memos is now a Ninth Circuit Justice."

"Great, just what I need."

"Well, our Colonel Masters served at Abu Ghraib."

"No shit?"

"No shit. And his right hand man was none other than…"

"Let me guess. Sergeant William Brown."

"I'm seeing a cover up here."

"It's not a cover up. It's a cover 'all the way up.'"

"You're right. I'm saving this one for rebuttal. Find out as much as you can about Masters and Brown."

"The sex experts?"

"That was Masters and Johnson."

"The law firm?"

"Be serious for once in your life."

"That would be no fun."

***

The next adverse witness Brent put up for his case in chief was Special Agent Ralph Jeffries, the lead FBI agent who coordinated the search of Catherine and Ahmed's home without notice. He identified the members of Jeffries's team and their function, and then tore right into him like a rabid dog.

"Special Agent Jeffries, your team conducted surveillance on Ahmed and Catherine Khury, is that correct?"

"Yes."

"When I refer to "you," Special Agent Jeffries, I am referring to you or any member of your team. When I say, "you personally," it means only you, okay?"

"Yes."

"You wiretapped Catherine and Ahmed's cell phones before Ahmed went to Iraq, isn't that correct?"

"Yes."

"And that was without a wiretap order to tap the Khury's cell phones in particular, correct?"

"We had a wiretap order."

"But that wiretap order was not a court issued order, was it?"

"It was a national security letter."

"Issued by the FBI, correct?"

"Yes."

"Sir, your national security letter order did not specify Ahmed or Catherine Khury, is that correct?"

"That is correct. It directed a roving wiretap relative to money laundering operations in Iraq of suspected al Qaeda operators."

"In this case, the roving wiretap was directed at Sabeen Khury, wasn't it?"

"Yes, it was."

"So when Sabeen made a phone call to the Khurys, you listened, correct?"

"Correct."

"And when he sent an email to Ahmed Khury, you intercepted their emails, correct?"

"Yes."

"You also secured Ahmed and Catherine Khury's credit report from Experian, Trans Union and Equifax, isn't that correct?"

"Yes."

"And that was without their permission, wasn't it?"

"We didn't need their permission."

"Move to strike as non-responsive. Answer the question, sir."

"Objection!" Nagel interjected.

"Objection sustained," said the judge, irritated with Brent's usurpation of his authority. "I will rule on the motions here, Mr. Marks. Agent Jeffries's answer is stricken. You will answer the question, Agent Jeffries."

"It was without their permission?"

"Yes."

"And without their knowledge?"

"Yes, without their knowledge."

"This national security letter issued by your bureau, it had a non-disclosure provision in it, didn't it?"

"Yes."

"And that non-disclosure provision prohibited the recipient from disclosing its existence, isn't that correct?"

"Yes."

"So, for example, Experian was prohibited from disclosing to the Khurys that their credit report was given to the FBI, correct?"

"That is correct."

"And Verizon was prohibited from disclosing to the Khurys that their telephones had been tapped, right?"

"Yes."

"And, on May 26, 2006, you entered the home of Catherine and Ahmed Khury, correct?"

"Yes."

"You did not announce yourselves, correct?"

"Correct."

"And you gained access to the home by having a locksmith pick the lock on their front door, correct?"

"Yes."

"This search was also authorized by the national security letter?"

"Yes."

"Without Catherine's permission?"

"Correct."

Brent guided the jury through the search of the Khury's home with Jeffries's testimony, disclosing every detail.

"And you left the home with photos of Ahmed from the Khury's family photo albums that you had seized?"

"Yes."

"And took a laptop and a PC from their home?"

"Yes."

"Again, without their permission?"

"Yes."

"And without a warrant?"

"Yes."

"Agent Jeffries, in all the material you took from the Khury home, you found no evidence that either Catherine or Ahmed Khury was involved in any terrorist activity, is that correct?"

"That is correct."

"And in all the records you examined that you obtained from the national security letter, you found no evidence that either Catherine or Ahmed Khury was involved in any terrorist activity, is that correct?"

"Correct."

"Agent Jeffries, finally, in all the telephone calls you intercepted, you found no evidence that either Catherine or Ahmed Khury was involved in any terrorist activity, is that correct?"

"We found communications with Sabeen Khury, a suspected terrorist."

"Move to strike as non-responsive. Answer the question please, sir."

"Granted, answer the question."

"That is correct."

"And in all the emails you intercepted, you found no evidence that Catherine or Ahmed Khury was involved in any terrorist activity, correct?"

"No, sir. We found emails to arrange meetings with Sabeen Khury, a suspected terrorist."

"You found emails to arrange a meeting with Ahmed Khury's brother?"

"Correct, in Iraq."

"Where both Sabeen and Ahmed Khury were born?"

"Yes."

"And where Sabeen Khury still lived?"

"Yes."

There was not much Nagel could hope to gain from cross-examining his own witness. Brent had spoiled his party by calling the witness for his own case, so Nagel just rolled with it and emphasized the points he wanted to make without unnecessary repetition of the damaging ones.

"Special Agent Jeffries, the national security letter you received from the FBI was part of an authorized international investigation into terrorism and clandestine intelligence activities, pursuant to the Foreign Intelligence Surveillance Act, as amended by Section 505 of the Patriot Act, isn't that correct?"

"Yes."

"So your team did nothing against the law in executing the order, right?"

"Objection!" Brent interrupted. "Calls for a legal conclusion."

"Sustained."

"Special Agent Jeffries, did you stay within the parameters of the national security letter?"

"Yes, we did."

"And was your department in possession of intelligence reports that showed a clear and present terrorist threat from Sabeen Khury?"

"Yes."

"Thank you. No further questions, Your Honor."

CHAPTER FORTY-SIX

Brent was beat up from the day at the trial and beat himself up more on the freeway on the long trip home. His eyelids felt like there were weights tied to the eyelashes, and he fought to stay alert. It would have been smarter to take a hotel downtown to avoid the trek. He wondered what it must be like for the thousands of people who made a one or two hour commute every day, because it was pure torture for him. When he arrived home, he could feel the blood pounding in his head, and every pulsation was painful. Opening the door, he raced the cat to the kitchen.

"Advil first, Calico."

In cattish selfishness, Calico mewed incessantly for her dinner. Every utterance seemed to create a new headache for Brent, who struggled to get the cap off the Advil, poured a glass of water hastily, and eagerly gulped down three tablets as if he was fulfilling his last dying wish. Then the phone rang.

"Fuck!" the expletive echoed against the walls, which made even the cat take a break from gulping her food.

"Hi honey!" It was Debbie, all happy and cheery.

"Hey Deb, I really can't talk right now."

"What's the matter? Calico got your tongue? Ha ha!"

Her lame attempt at humor was not even mildly amusing for Brent.

"Yes, ha ha," he said in a 'courtesy laugh.' "I really have to go, Debbie, I'm not feeling well."

"What's wrong?" Her curiosity demanded a medical explanation inevitably leading to more unnecessary conversation that could not possibly help his headache.

"Got a headache. Can I call you back in a while?"

"Sure."

Brent hung up and slumped into his living room chair. "I hate the goddamn phone," he said to the cat, who looked up at him with curiosity, swished her tail, and then rubbed against his leg in gratitude for her dinner.

He checked with the office: Forty-five unanswered messages. The financial pressure he was experiencing by neglecting attention to his other cases and concentrating on the trial had built up, complicated by the fact that he, and not Catherine Khury, had been paying all the expert witness fees and jury fees. Rick was taking his investigative fees on the come.

Brent slumped back in his chair and waited for the Advil to take effect. Mental exhaustion resulted in his dozing off a bit, which was never known by him to be a good cure for a headache, but obviously his body needed it.

He awoke from the nap to a rapping at the door. Rising and grumbling, Brent approached the door and opened it.

"Surprise!" It was Debbie.

"Deb, I'm not much in the mood for surprises."

Debbie pushed Brent aside gently and came in. "I have just what you need," she said. After a warm bath, a massage and some intimate personal attention, Brent agreed and decided to write the maker of Advil to complain.

CHAPTER FORTY-SEVEN

Brent had to squeeze two more expert witnesses in, so he saved the most interesting one for last, and first called Marvin Ketzler, an actuary and fellow of the Society of Actuaries and member of the American Academy of Actuaries. Ketzler had spent 25 years in the insurance industry in risk assessment. He couldn't tell you if anyone was a good person or not, but he could tell you within $100 of what he or she was worth in dollars and cents.

Ketzler testified that, had his life not ended as it did, Ahmed Khury would have, most likely, lived to be at least 85.4 years old, and would have had another 32 years of gainful employment ahead of him as an accountant. He calculated his future salary, discounted it for the future value of money, and calculated that, in dollars and cents, Ahmed was worth $5.9 million to his family.

The next witness in Brent's case in chief was Doctor Stephen Ransen, a forensic psychologist. Dr. Ransen took the witness chair and talked to the jury in a very unassuming bedside manner. He outlined his 42 years' experience in the field, his medical degree, psychiatric residency, that he was a Diplomate in Psychiatry and Forensic Psychiatry, and the fact that he was also a Qualified Medical Examiner in the state of California. Dr. Ransen had authored over 60 articles, including those on suicide prevention, and had an impressive alphabet soup collection of professional affiliations.

"Dr. Ransen, you were hired by the Plaintiff to make an assessment on the mental condition that led to Ahmed Khury's suicide, is that correct?"

"Yes."

"Can you outline for the jury, please, what facts you have examined in order to make that assessment?"

"Certainly."

From that point on, Brent was just a bystander, as Dr. Ransen took over the jury mind, body and soul. He made eye contact with each and every member, and spoke in a calm, reassuring, almost hypnotic tone.

"I have been listening to the testimony of the witnesses the past three days concerning the conditions Mr. Khury endured while detained. I have also examined both autopsy reports, all reports of his medical condition while incarcerated, as well as his historical medical reports before incarceration."

"Doctor, from your examination of all the evidence, have you been able to form an opinion, within a reasonable medical certainty, of the cause of Mr. Khury's suicide, if it in fact, was a suicide?"

"Yes, I have."

"Can you please explain that opinion and your basis for it to the jury?"

"Yes, of course. From my examination of the evidence, I am not entirely convinced that Mr. Khury took his own life. I concur with the opinion of Dr. Orozco. However, there is evidence of suicidal impulses on the part of Mr. Khury, and it is my opinion that these impulses were not controllable by Mr. Khury and were the result of a mental condition caused by the treatment of his jailers."

Dr. Ransen explained studies to the jury, in layman's terms, of the effect of solitary confinement, sensory deprivation, and sensory overstimulation on psychiatric syndromes.

"These studies point out in detail what psychiatrists have known for a long time: that severe restriction of environmental and social stimulation has a profound deleterious effect on mental functioning. That solitary confinement was purposely used to "break down" Mr. Khury mentally so that he would be susceptible to the enhanced interrogation techniques that have been described in court is extremely troubling.

"But Mr. Khury did not only experience solitary confinement. He was purposely deprived of all sensory input for long periods of time, as a perfectly acceptable form of treatment by his captors. This treatment, which was specifically aimed at making him mentally dependent on his interrogators, contributed to his unstable mental condition.

"Observations in the numerous studies have shown common features in cases of sensory deprivation, such as intense desire for extrinsic sensory stimuli and bodily motion, increased suggestibility, impairment of organized thinking, oppression and depression, and, in extreme cases, hallucinations, delusions, and confusion.

"After even a brief time of sensory deprivation, a normal individual is likely to descend into a mental torpor. This is like a blanket of fog that comes over your mind, and impairs alertness, attention and concentration.

316

"An individual subjected to long periods of sensory deprivation becomes incapable of processing external stimuli, and becomes hyper-responsive, overreacting to any kind of sensory stimulation. Over time, the complete absence of stimulation causes any stimulus to become noxious and annoying. For example, if I clapped my hands like this, normally you would not find that too annoying. If, however, you were subjected to that noise after a long period of sensory deprivation, you may find it to be unbearable."

"Doctor, does the fact that Mr. Khury was not only subjected to sensory deprivation, but also long periods of sensory overstimulation affect your opinion?"

"Yes, there are a number of studies on the effect of sensory overload on the mental state."

Dr. Ransen went on to outline the findings of the medical articles on sensory overload. As he spoke, Brent watched the jury to make sure that they would not be lost in the medical mumbo jumbo that doctors tend to engage in, but Ransen broke it down to the lowest common denominators.

"These results of cognitive and intellectual impairment from sensory overload are exacerbated by the sensory deprivation Mr.

Khury experienced. Imagine coming from an environment with absolutely no outside stimuli, which, as I stated before, makes an individual hypersensitive to any tiny stimulation, to being bombarded with loud noise and bright lights for 24 hours a day.

"The psychological effect of such overstimulation is devastating. The exposure of Mr. Khury to the type of treatment he experienced at the hands of his captors reasonably led to uncontrollable impulses to commit suicide on his part."

"Dr. Ransen, do you have an opinion, within a reasonable degree of medical certainty, as to whether a reasonable person would perceive Mr. Khury's treatment to create a danger to his medical condition?"

"Yes, I do. It is my opinion that, not only did his captors treat Mr. Khury with deliberate indifference to his expressions of suicidal tendencies, but also they were actually trained in the techniques they used and knew that they were being used to break him down mentally. Further, they knew that these techniques were dangerous."

"Objection and move to strike!" barked Nagel. "Lack of foundation!"

"Overruled."

"Doctor, how do you know that they knew these techniques were dangerous?" Brent asked, moving in for the kill.

"If what you have heard in the past three days has turned your stomach as much as it has mine, imagine what the jailers, who actually witnessed the cruel and heartless treatment Mr. Khury was subjected to thought. And imagine how it would be to inflict such misery on another person day after day and be hardened to the point of indifference. If my dog were treated the way Mr. Khury was, I might be compelled to commit murder, Mr. Marks."

"Objection! Move to strike as prejudicial."

"Overruled."

Each juror's face was frozen in shock, and no matter how Nagel plotted and schemed to twist the testimony of Dr. Ransen his way, he knew that it would not diminish the emotional effect that it had on the jurors. The knockout punch having been delivered, it was time for Brent to rest his case.

PART IV

THE WAR ON TERROR

CHAPTER FORTY-EIGHT

Timothy Nagel had an enormous job ahead of him. He had to convince the jury that everything that they had heard was all necessary in the interests of national security, and that their safety depended on treating detainees in the manner in which Ahmed had been treated. It was a formidable task, but not impossible. Nagel only had 12 people to sway. George Bush had already convinced 100 senators and 435 Congressmen to obliterate 200 years of constitutionally-guaranteed freedoms for the sake of national security.

Brent had already tried Nagel's case to a certain extent, by calling his star witnesses as adverse witnesses for the Plaintiff. But Nagel had saved his secret weapons for his own presentation. He called Captain James Billings, a reserve officer in the army, as his first witness. Brent was sure that Billings' naval career was merely a CIA front to hide his real assignment, but there was no way to prove it.

"Captain Billings, what is your current rank and assignment with the U.S. Army Reserve?"

"I am a special investigator for United States Army Military Intelligence Corps, currently serving as a reserve officer."

"As such, were you assigned to interrogate Ahmed Khury at the Guantanamo Bay Detention Camp 7?"

"I was."

"Please describe to the jury the circumstances of that interrogation."

Billings was smooth and cool, like the expert witness doctors who had testified before him. He sized up the jury right away, and made eye contact with them.

"Certainly. I was assigned an investigative file on Ahmed Khury, who was captured along with his brother, Sabeen Khury, a suspected money launderer for al Qaeda. I was one of a two-man joint investigative group assigned to interrogate Mr. Khury at Guantanamo Bay."

"And who was the other member of the group?"

"Captain Louis Rapallo."

"Was anyone other than Captain Rapallo with you in the room when you interrogated Mr. Khury?"

"No."

"Captain Billings, in your interrogation of Mr. Khury, did you use any enhanced interrogation techniques?"

"No."

"Captain Billings, do you know what waterboarding is?"

"Yes."

"Did you use waterboarding?"

"No."

Finally, after about 40 minutes of waterboarding, which seemed like a lifetime to Ahmed, the next time the cloth came off, Ahmed spit, sucked in air and screamed, "Please stop, I'll tell you everything!" He couldn't take any more and had decided to tell them everything they wanted to hear.

"He needed your help with his money laundering operation?"

"Yes!"

"For al Qaeda?"

"Yes!"

"And you met members of al Qaeda with your brother?"

"Yes!"

"Who did you meet? What are their names?"

Ahmed looked into the serious dead eyes of the two clean cut, shaven, non-military men. He was sure if he didn't give them some names, they would kill him. The names couldn't be just names. They had to go with faces. He thought of the few people he had met with his brother in Baghdad. Am I condemning these men to death? *he questioned himself.*

"Ali Bahar, Kasim Ghannam, and Mahmod Handal."

"Is that all?"

"Yes."

"Very good Haji, very good!" said Sergeant Brown, in the background. "You just may live another day."

"Captain Billings, how long did your interrogation of Mr. Khury last?"

"The initial interrogation was eight hours long."

"And was Mr. Khury given the opportunity to go to the toilet during the interrogation?"

"Yes."

"I have to go to the toilet," pleaded Ahmed.

"You will have the opportunity to go when we're done," said one of the strangers.

"But I can't hold it any longer!"

"Don't you piss your pants again, Haji," said Sergeant Brown. I told you before, we're not a laundry service."

"Was Mr. Khury given water for hydration during the interrogation?"

"He was offered water, but refused. So we had to have a naval nurse give him an IV."

"Was he offered food during the interrogation?"

"He was, but he refused to eat."

The cloth finally came off again, and Ahmed spit out water, choked and gasped for air.

"What do you know about al Qaeda's plans to move money out of Iraq?"

"I told you before, I don't know anything!"

"Mr. Khury, would you like a glass of water to drink?"

"What? Are you kidding?"

"If you refuse water, we will have to give you fluids intravenously."

"Captain Billings, was your interrogation of Mr. Khury audiotaped?"

"Yes."

"Was the tape transcribed into a transcript?"

"Yes."

"Showing you what has been marked for identification as Exhibit number 52, can you identify this document?"

"It's the transcript of the interrogation."

"Move Exhibit 52 into evidence, Your Honor."

"Objection!" said Brent. Hearsay, res judicata, and best evidence."

"Counsel approach the bench."

"Your Honor, in the habeas corpus proceeding, you threw out the confession as coerced," pleaded Brent.

"Your Honor," said Nagel, "I'm not offering it for the truth of the matters set forth in the transcript. Only as evidence of the treatment that Mr. Khury received at the hands of his interrogators."

"You opened the door, Counsel," said Judge Henley.

"Your Honor, if this comes in, then I should have the opportunity to introduce my client's sworn statement of the treatment he received at the hands of his interrogators."

"Your Honor, that is an out-of-court statement that the Government did not have the opportunity to cross-examine," objected Nagel.

"I offer it for the limited purpose of impeaching this witness," said Brent.

"Your Honor, it contains hearsay within hearsay, and is too prejudicial to admit since we did not have the opportunity to cross-examine."

"I'm afraid he's right, Mr. Marks."

"So this transcript of what they say happened comes in, and Mr. Khury's does not, is that what you're saying, Your Honor?"

"I'm afraid so."

"My ruling is that the transcript may be admitted into evidence. Identification and admission of Plaintiff's proposed exhibit for impeachment, which is the declaration of Ahmed Khury from the habeas corpus proceeding, is denied pursuant to Rule 402 of the Federal Rules of Evidence."

It was a huge blow to Brent's case. Now the jury would see the doctored and bogus transcript and would not even see Ahmed's version of what happened in that interrogation room. As Brent was heading back to the counsel table, he saw that strange young man in the back of the gallery, smirking at him. The look in his eyes was wild and made Brent feel uncomfortable.

"Captain Billings, did you conduct a second interview of Mr. Khury?"

"Yes, two weeks later we conducted a follow-up interview."

"Showing you what has been marked for identification as Exhibit number 53, is this a true and accurate transcript of that interview?"

"Yes, it is."

"Move Exhibit 53 into evidence, Your Honor."

"Same objection, Your Honor."

"Overruled."

The wind had been taken out of Brent's sails. He dared not even cross-examine Billings, because he had already lied about waterboarding and dry-boarding, and had done it coolly and calmly, without changing his expression. He was a terrific liar, and the cardinal rule of cross-examination was never to ask a question that you did not know how the witness would answer. Brent could not run the risk of making him look even better.

Nagel called Louis Rapallo to the stand, who testified, in clone-like fashion, in the exact same manner and as to the same facts as Billings. They had gotten their stories straight, and with precision. Napoleon said, "History is a set of lies agreed upon." There was nothing that Brent could do at this point to rewrite history for the jury.

CHAPTER FORTY-NINE

Colonel Robert Masters took the stand. Brent imagined how the jury would see him. Twenty years of military service had imprinted itself on the Colonel's soul. It defined him. He was as stiff as a starched shirt, but, somehow, for him, that appeared to be normal.

Nagel had Masters describe the chain of command in Camp 7, and Masters was at the top of it. He answered to a General in Camp Delta, and was left to handle Camp 7 as he saw fit.

"Colonel Masters, can you please describe Camp 7?"

"Camp 7 is a classified, high security detention facility, used to house high value detainees. Due to the fact that it is classified, I cannot disclose its location or layout."

"What do you mean by "high value detainees"?

"High value detainees are those who are the 'worst of the worst.' The types who have been accused of the 1998 Embassy bombings, the USS Cole bombing, planning the September 11th attacks…"

"Dangerous people."

"Yes."

"What kinds of precautions are taken in Camp 7 that are different than in the other detention facilities at Guantanamo?"

"The location of the camp is a strictly held secret. Detainees being moved from the Camp to other locations, such as military tribunals, or classified areas within the facility must wear blackout hoods to ensure the secrecy and integrity of the facility. Because the facility contains such high value and dangerous detainees, when detainees are moved, a special armed detail of guards are used to ensure the safety of personnel and to prevent escape."

"Is torture ever practiced on detainees?"

"Absolutely not. Our standard operating manual prohibits torture. Detainees are treated within the spirit of the Geneva Conventions."

∗∗∗

Brent pulled Rick aside at the break.

"So who is that little fuck who sits in the back of the gallery every day and just loves it when I'm losing?"

"His name is Theodore Anderson. U.S. Marine Corps Corporal. Was part of a unit of guards at Gitmo during his last tour, but they transferred him."

"Why?"

"He's not exactly the calmest one in the bunch. Beat one of his comrades nearly to death in a fight for not being a good patriot. Not enough evidence for a court martial. Nobody would talk. They call him Balls, because he's not afraid of anybody."

"Now you tell me."

"Don't worry, I've got your back. I can't connect him to the case. Looks like just a nut who wants you to lose this one, that's all."

"Well, keep an eye on him. He gives me the creeps."

***

"What precautions are taken when detainees show suicidal tendencies?" asked Nagel.

"If a detainee is suspected of being suicidal, he is referred to the psychiatric hospital for a suicide evaluation. If determined to be suicidal, he is issued special bed sheets and blankets that cannot be torn or tied."

"Was Mr. Khury suspected as suicidal?"

"No, but he was referred for a psych eval because of comments that he had made to staff."

"What comments were those?"

"That he would be better off dead than in this place, things like that. Things everyone has been known to say in their life from time to time. We just prefer to err on the side of precaution."

"And, after hearing those comments, what did you do?"

"We referred him to a psychiatric evaluation, with negative results."

"Did you take any other precautions?"

"Yes, he was placed on a one to three minute check, meaning that every one to three minutes, a guard would look into his cell."

Colonel Masters picked up his radio.

"Masters."

"Colonel, it's Sergeant Brown. We got a situation here."

"What is it, Sergeant?"

"This Haji-Ahab...Khury...He was being force-fed and stopped breathing."

"Did you try to revive him?"

"Yes, sir."

"The nurse is there?"

"Yes, sir."

"Is he dead, Sergeant?"

"Yes, sir."

"Well, all I can say is handle it. We can't have a dead Haji in the feeding room."

"Handle it, sir?"

"Make sure he's found somewhere else, Sergeant, is that clear?"

"Yes, sir."

"Were you surprised when he was found hanging in his cell, the victim of an apparent suicide?"

"Yes, I was."

"No further questions, Your Honor."

"Mr. Marks?"

"Thank you, Your Honor. Colonel Masters, before your assignment at Camp 7, what was your assignment?"

"I was assigned to Camp Delta in 2003."

"And before Camp Delta, isn't it true that you were assigned to duty at the Abu Ghraib prison in Iraq?"

"Yes, sir."

Nagel looked at Masters like someone had just kicked him in the balls. He obviously didn't know this fundamental part of Masters's history.

"This is the same Abu Ghraib prison that was the subject of a criminal investigation by the United States Army Criminal Investigation Command for prisoner abuse, which found that guards in Abu Ghraib prison had physically and sexually abused, tortured, raped, sodomized, and killed prisoners?"

"Objection!" said Nagel. "May we approach?"

"Your objection, Mr. Nagel?"

"Rule 420, Your Honor, prejudicial effect of this testimony outweighs its probative value."

"He's your witness and this is cross examination, Mr. Nagel. I'm going to allow it."

"Sergeant Brown served under your command at Abu Ghraib, didn't he?" Brent continued.

"Yes, sir."

Nagel turned slightly to Joe Cicatto and frowned and grimaced slightly, like he had just smelled a fart. He made a mental note to tear Joe a new asshole once they got out of the courtroom.

"Colonel, were you under investigation for prisoner abuse at Abu Ghraib?"

"Objection, Your Honor. Inadmissible character evidence."

"Sustained." Too late: the point had already been made to the jury. Nagel probably should have let that one go. He had no idea, but a "no" answer was coming and his objection made it look like he was hiding something.

Brent turned his head and winked to Rick, who flashed back a satisfying, but subtle smile. The day, which had started with disaster, looked to be ending on a good note.

CHAPTER FIFTY

Brent felt his nose twitching, and unconsciously went to scratch it with his finger. It happened again, and again, and he rolled over on the couch. Calico persistently jumped over his body into the crook of his arm until she could reach his face and began pawing again.

"What the hell?" Brent awoke, startled, to Calico's purring engine. It was only 8 pm, and he had dozed off in the midst of going over his notes. "I guess my first mistress really is the law," he said to the cat, as he yawned and stretched, and Calico joined him. "Somehow, your yawns seem like so much more fun," he exclaimed, as she stretched three cat lengths, opened her mouth, and let it rip.

Brent realized that he had forgotten his dinner with Debbie Does Dallas, so he popped up from the couch to get ready. The familiar growl in his stomach told him that going out was the right decision. Since the trial, his home provisions had dwindled to cat food, eggs, mayonnaise and ketchup and, while that sounded like the beginnings of a terrific new experimental recipe, the idea of fajitas with fresh guacamole topped off with a margarita sounded better.

Brent picked up Debbie and they headed for El Paseo on Anacapa Street. As the music played in time to the tinkling fountain in the middle of the courtyard and the margaritas flowed, Brent actually began to relax.

"I could get used to this," he said.

"There is more to life than law."

"My mentor, Charles Stinson, is turning over in his grave at that statement."

"Why?"

"Because, during a trial, the trial *is* your life. Nothing else matters."

"How's it going?"

"Terrible. We're on their case in chief now, and it's almost impossible to cross-examine a good liar."

"What about a bad one?"

"Haven't run into one on this case, except for Corporal Reeding. He changed his testimony since I deposed him. I think someone got to him."

"A cover up?"

"Yeah, I'm thinking all the way up, but with their military code of silence, nobody's talking. I'm afraid the truth will never be known. But, whether it is or not, the jury will decide what they think happened."

"What are your chances of winning?"

"If I had to guess right now, I'd say 50-50."

"A hung jury?"

"Hope not."

They decided to walk home to Debbie's house, which was close to downtown. It was a pleasant night, with a full moon transforming the night sky into cobalt blue, above the twinkling lights of State Street. As they passed Brent's office, he turned his head and instinctively tried to go into the front entrance. Debbie steered him in the other direction.

"Not now, Mr. Workaholic. You've got to walk this lady home."

"With pleasure." Brent gave Debbie his arm and they continued to her little bungalow on Anapamu.

"Want to come in?" she asked, as they paused at her doorstep.

Brent leaned in for a kiss, which was met with equal enthusiasm, causing a rush of hormones that would lead him on a one-way path.

"Raincheck?" he murmured almost helplessly, as she kissed him back passionately, and he felt the warmth of her soft body against his.

"You sure?" she asked, as Brent stroked her cheek and dived in for another round.

"Well, maybe for a while."

Brent thought of the famous quote from the movie, *Arthur*; "Isn't fun the best thing to have?" He could get used to this "relationship thing." For some reason or another, any relationship he had ever formed with a member of the opposite sex did not last too long. Maybe "Debbie Does Dallas" was not so bad for him after all.

CHAPTER FIFTY-ONE

Lieutenant Commander Michael Farraday was the medical examiner from NCIS who had performed the first autopsy on Ahmed. Most people are intimidated by doctors, and you would think the jurors would be even more intimidated by one in a crisp naval officer's uniform, but Doctor Farraday had a surprisingly good bedside manner that you would not expect from a doctor whose patients could have never benefited from it, because of the fact that they were all deceased. He spoke to the jury in a calm, reassuring, but authoritative way. He was a pleasant looking, handsome Dr. Kildaire type, as opposed to Dr. Orozco, who could be regarded as something of a slob.

"Doctor Farraday, can you please tell the jury a little about your background and experience?"

"Of course. This can get a little boring Ladies and Gentlemen, so I apologize in advance." Dr. Farraday smiled a pleasant smile, and delivered his "I am super doctor" speech to them with deliberate articulation. Like Dr. Orozco, Farraday had an impressive set of credentials, and he was younger and better looking, an irrelevant point to anyone else but the jury, who would put as much value on his appearance as his testimony.

"I am a certified medical examiner, currently serving with the Naval Criminal Investigative Service. I hold an M.D. and a PhD from Georgetown University School of Medicine, an A.B. from Dartmouth, and a medical license from the State of Virginia, where I am board certified in clinical, anatomic and forensic pathology. I am a Diplomate of the American Board of Forensic Medicine. I did my residency at the University of Florida Health Sciences Center, my general medicine internship at the Naval Medical Center in San Diego, California, and received aerospace medicine specialty training at the Naval Aerospace Medical Institute in Pensacola, Florida. I served as a naval flight surgeon for 6 years at the Marine Air Corps Station in Beaufort, South

Carolina, and served as a Medical Education and Training Officer there for six years, before assuming my present position as a medical examiner for NCIS, where I have performed over 3,000 autopsies over the past 15 years. I have also published numerous medical journal articles, which are listed in my curriculum vitae. Sorry if that seemed to be one enormous, continuous sentence."

Members of the jury smiled and there was one chuckle. They were in love with him.

"Doctor Farraday," said Nagel, handing him a piece of paper, "Can you identify what has been marked for identification as Exhibit 54?"

"Yes, this is my curriculum vitae."

"Move Exhibit 54 into evidence, Your Honor."

"No objection? It is received."

"Doctor Farraday, you read the expert report of Doctor Jaime Orozco, did you not?"

"Yes, I did."

"And did you agree with Dr. Orozco's opinion on the cause of death?"

"No, I did not."

"Can you tell the jury why?"

"Although there was some evidence of aspiration of a small amount of fluid in Mr. Khury's case that is fairly common in enteral feeding. It is my opinion that the small amount of fluid aspirated was not enough to cause death. The forensic evidence in his case was consistent with asphyxiation by hanging."

"What about Dr. Orozco's comments on the lack of ligature marks consistent with death by hanging, and the lack of abrasions or hemorrhages in the skin and indeed, no hemorrhages in the eyes?"

"First of all, Ladies and Gentlemen," Farraday said, making eye contact with the members of the jury, "The presence of ligature marks depends on the composition of the ligature. In this case, it was a soft cotton and rayon jumpsuit leg sleeve. This type of ligature does not often leave a mark, or will leave only a superficial one.

"Further, the presence of the mark may be affected by the amount of time the body was suspended. It takes only 2 kilograms of tension to close the jugular veins and only 15 kilograms tension to close the trachea. Death by asphyxiation happens quickly, in no more than three minutes. In this case, when cells are monitored every one to three minutes, the body was discovered relatively quickly after death."

"What about the use of olive oil as a lubricant? Would that cause you to change your opinion?"

"Not at all. As Doctor Orozco stated, lipoid pneumonia was not the cause of death, and I concur. Lipoid pneumonia cannot cause death in such a short period of time."

"Dr. Farraday, you performed the first autopsy on Mr. Khury, is that correct?"

"Yes."

"And Dr. Orozco performed a second autopsy?"

"Correct."

"Are there any limitations on a second autopsy in this case?"

"Yes. Ladies and Gentlemen, an autopsy should take place as soon as possible after death. The best evidence is available at the first autopsy, because, since the body begins to decompose rapidly from the lack of oxygen, time is your enemy.

"Although second autopsies are not per se considered unreliable, in this case, Dr. Orozco did not have the chance to dissect the internal organs for examination, and he couldn't examine the body fluids because they had already been removed, examined and disposed of. He only had preserved tissue samples to refer to, which makes his examination secondary to the autopsy that I performed."

"So doctor, in your opinion, because of all those reasons you have articulated, were you able to make a more thorough and pertinent examination than Dr. Orozco?"

"Yes, I was."

"Doctor, do you have an opinion within a degree of reasonable medical certainty, of the cause of Mr. Khury's death?"

"Yes. It is my opinion that the cause of Mr. Khury's death was asphyxiation by hanging in an apparent suicide."

"And do you have an opinion as to whether Mr. Khury's death was the result of gross negligent medical care in his last enteral feeding?"

"Yes. It is my opinion that his death was not a proximate result of gross negligent medical practices or reckless disregard of standard medical practices."

Again, in the back in the gallery, Balls Anderson sat in his usual place, smirking, as if he was sitting in his living room, watching a ridiculous reality TV show.

CHAPTER FIFTY-TWO

Now it was Brent's task to engage the doctor in cross-examination, which was going to be like an intellectual chess game, with the odds stacked in favor of the doctor due to Brent's lack of medical expertise.

Brent didn't have time to go over the testimony with Dr. Orozco to prepare, but they both knew that the Navy doctor would come up with a perfectly plausible explanation that his opinion was the correct one. It was important to emphasize any weaknesses in that opinion so the jury didn't end up tossing a coin in the jury room during their deliberations.

"Dr. Faraday, when you said you disagreed with Dr. Orozco's opinion, that means you have a different opinion than he does, isn't that correct?"

"Yes, it is."

"And Dr. Orozco's opinion is a completely different opinion of what caused Mr. Khury's death, right?"

"Yes."

"Now, doctor, between your and Dr. Orozco, you think that your opinion is the correct one, don't you?"

Farraday smiled and said, "Of course it is." The jury caught his infectious smile. This guy was good.

"Move to strike as non-responsive, Your Honor."

"Granted."

"Could you please repeat the question?" Farraday knew full well what the question was. He just wanted to emphasize his innocence and impartiality.

"Yes. Between your opinion and Dr. Orozco's opinion, you think that your opinion is the right one, don't you?"

"I think that, within reasonable medical certainty that my opinion is correct and Dr. Orozco's is not correct, yes." That was not exactly an answer to the question, but Brent had to live with it. Still, it was worth a shot to try to put him in his place.

"Move to strike everything but "yes", Your Honor."

"Denied. Please continue, Mr. Marks."

"Isn't it also true, Dr. Farraday, that Dr. Orozco's opinion is based, in part, on the forensic evidence in the report from the autopsy you performed?"

Farraday paused for a moment. He didn't want to find himself checkmated. "He stated that his opinion was so based, yes."

"Move to strike as non-responsive, Your Honor."

"Granted. Please answer the question, doctor."

"Yes, his opinion appeared to be based, at least in part on the forensic evidence in my autopsy report."

"And it was also based on his own examination, correct?"

"Yes."

"And you did not perform a second autopsy on the body of Mr. Khury, did you?"

"There was no need."

"Move to strike as non-responsive, Your Honor."

"Granted, please answer the question, doctor."

"No I did not."

"So Dr. Orozco's opinion then, is based on your report as well as his own examination, and yours is based solely on your report, is that correct?"

"Objection! Compound and argumentative!" barked Nagel, weighing in on the game.

"Sustained."

No matter, thought Brent. The jury had heard the conclusion he made and some were nodding their heads in agreement.

The intellectual tug of war continued for about an hour, and Brent was careful to try to paint Farraday into a corner whenever he could, as opposed to allowing him to pontificate on how superior his opinion was to Dr. Orozco's. Nagel then went into redirect.

***

By that time, at least one member in the jury was nodding off, which signaled that their joint attention span was wearing thin and in serious need of a junk food recharge. Thankfully, within walking distance of the courthouse was the L.A. Mall, filled with a delectable choice of nutritious meals, from Carl's, Jr. to Quiznos. Brent and Rick settled on the less noxious California Pita.

Out of the corner of his eye, Brent saw Balls Anderson, sitting at a corner table.

"That little fucker is following us," he said to Rick.

"I'll go have a talk with him."

Rick got up, sauntered over to Balls' table, and sat down. Balls looked at him with those crazy eyes.

"Hello, sir."

"Hello, Balls." Balls looked surprised that someone knew his nickname.

"How do you know my nickname?"

"I'm an ex G-Man, Balls, nothing gets past me."

"What do you want?"

"We're trying to have a privileged conversation here. You're too close."

"It's a public place. I have the right to eat here, sir."

"Not if you're stalking us, you don't. You know what's up there?" Rick asked, pointing at the ceiling.

"What?"

"L.A.P.D. station. I wonder how fun your lunch would be if a couple of uniformed officers came down here to put you in a crime report. Does your command even know you're here?"

"I'm on leave."

"So, leave then." Rick signaled with his thumb for Balls to "hit the road." Balls got up, leaving his uneaten lunch on the table.

"This isn't over," he said, and walked away.

Punching his buttons may have not been the brightest thing to do, but Rick knew from experience that it was the only way to pop open a lead that wasn't leading anywhere. He just had to make sure to keep a keener eye on Brent. It looked like the timer on Balls' fuse had just been activated.

CHAPTER FIFTY-THREE

Dr. Richard Lester's credentials as a clinical and forensic psychiatrist were beyond reproach. He held a PhD from Johns Hopkins University and an MD from Georgetown University School of Medicine, where he completed his internal medicine internship. He had completed his psychiatric residency at Johns Hopkins as well as a forensic psychiatry fellowship there.

Dr. Lester was a member of the American Psychiatric Association, the American Academy of Psychiatry and the Law, and the American Medical Association. He had written numerous articles in psychiatric, medical and law review journals, and had testified in court as an expert many hundreds of times. Lester had served as a Professor at several East Coast universities and medical schools. He was a Diplomate of the American Board of Psychiatry and Neurology with added qualifications in Forensic Psychiatry, and a Certified Forensic Physician with the American College of Forensic Examiners Institute.

"Dr. Lester," asked Nagel. "Just to be clear, you have been hired by the defense and paid for being here today to give your testimony, haven't you?"

"Yes, I have."

"But doctor, in the many times you have testified in the past, has it always been for the defense?"

"Oh, no, I have testified for the plaintiff's side many times. Each case is different, and I am always called upon to give impartial testimony."

"How many of those cases that you testified would you estimate were plaintiff's cases?"

"About 35%."

Dr. Lester testified as to the reports he reviewed, including Dr. Ransen's report, which he disagreed with.

"Dr. Lester, as a result of your review, have you been able to formulate an opinion, within a reasonable degree of medical certainty, whether the conditions of detention of Ahmed Khury resulted in a mental condition that contributed to his suicide?"

"Yes. It is my opinion that Mr. Khury could not have developed such a mental condition as a result of the conditions of his detention alone."

"Why?"

"While it is true that long periods of solitary confinement, sensory deprivation and overstimulation may exacerbate certain psychic syndromes, Mr. Khury's medical history was devoid of any mental conditions that could have been worsened by those conditions. Further, his solitary confinement was of too short a period to cause any serious mental effects."

"Doctor, does the fact that Mr. Khury was not only subjected to sensory deprivation, but also long periods of sensory overstimulation affect your opinion?"

"No. While I agree with Dr. Ransen that there are studies on the effects of sensory overload on the mental state, the period of time that Mr. Khury was subjected to this as part of his behavioral modification program was not significant as to cause any such effects."

Dr. Lester explained, in detail, the pathology of suicide, and how it was not likely that anyone, even a psychiatrist, could have predicted or prevented Ahmed's suicide, based on the information that was available.

"Suicide is a complex behavior, influenced by multiple synaptic systems, the functioning of which can be permanently altered by experience. The expression of a suicidal thought is rather common among humans, and does not necessarily lead to an attempt. Still, the precautions that were taken in Mr. Khury's case were reasonable, given the fact that the only symptom was the expression of a suicidal thought, given his lack of a previous mental conditions and lack of previous attempts."

"In your opinion, doctor, could the type of treatment Mr. Khury experienced during his detention reasonably lead to uncontrollable impulses to commit suicide?"

"No, it could not."

"Dr. Lester, do you have an opinion, within a reasonable degree of medical certainty, as to whether a reasonable person would perceive Mr. Khury's treatment to create a danger to his medical condition?"

"Yes, I do.   It is my opinion that a reasonable person would not perceive Mr. Khury's treatment to create any type of danger to his medical condition."

"Do you have an opinion as to whether the techniques used in the behavior modification program with Mr. Khury were used with deliberate indifference to his expressions of suicidal tendencies?"

"Yes. It is my opinion that the staff reacted reasonably in response to Mr. Khury's expressions and not with deliberate indifference."

Now that the jury was completely confused by conflicting testimonies from two different psychiatrists, Brent had the onerous job of cross-examination without confusing the jury even more.

CHAPTER FIFTY-FOUR

If engaging Dr. Farraday was a challenge, then the cross-examination of Dr. Lester proved to be even more of one, as Brent had to avoid the pitfall of attacking the field of psychiatry itself and its lack of reliability.

In Brent's dues-paying days, he sometimes took on personal injury cases, something he would not do now even if his practice depended on it. About ten years ago, a new psychiatrist moved to Santa Barbara and began doing evaluations for some insurance companies. In Brent's analysis of his potential new personal injury clients, they fit one of three types: a group of people that had absolutely nothing wrong with them; a group of pathological liars, and a group that Brent was convinced had something very wrong with them. Brent figured that he either had a black hole above his office, sucking in all the bad clients and depositing them in his waiting room, or there was something seriously wrong with the doctor.

Since Brent was relying on his own psychiatrist to cross over the finish line in case the jury did not buy the death by force-feeding and cover-up scenario, he dared not attack the science of psychiatry itself. However, Rick had done a thorough background check on Dr. Lester, and had come up with a nice slam dunk for Brent. No chess game this time: Brent would trip up Lester with his own words.

"Dr. Lester, you testified that about 35% of the cases you testified were cases in which the plaintiff hired you, is that correct?"

"Yes."

"Would it surprise you, doctor, if that number were a lot lower?"

"Why, yes, it would."

"Your honor, I have marked for identification as Exhibit 77, a list of all the federal and state cases in which Dr. Lester has testified. Its companion, Exhibit 78, is a spread sheet, showing those cases in which Dr. Lester has been hired by the plaintiff, and those in which he was hired by the defendant."

"Objection, Your Honor, I have not been provided with a copy of these exhibits in discovery," said Nagel.

"Counsel, please approach the bench."

"Mr. Marks, why has the defense not been provided copies of these exhibits?" asked Henley.

"They are for impeachment, Your Honor. They weren't relevant until he testified today."

"What is your offer of proof?"

"Dr. Lester testified that 35% of his cases were plaintiff's cases. The real number is a little less than 2%."

"Your honor, this is not relevant. I move that the exhibits be excluded per rule 403. It's too prejudicial," said Nagel.

"Motion denied, Mr. Nagel. It shows possible bias."

"Dr. Lester, please examine Exhibits 77 and 78."

"Very well." Lester got out his reading glasses and looked through the exhibits. Then, he indicated he had finished his review.

"Dr. Lester, does Exhibit 77 appear to be a list of the federal and state cases in which you have testified?"

"The cases look familiar. I'm sure they are mine, but what I'm not sure of is whether it is a complete list."

"My investigator, Richard Penn, compiled this list from a complete record of all the cases you have ever testified in, be it federal or state courts, since the beginning of your practice. Would it surprise you that the percentage of plaintiff's cases in which you have testified is considerably less than 35%?"

"Yes, it would."

"In fact, Exhibit 78 is a spreadsheet of the cases in Exhibit 77, and it shows that a little less than 2% of the cases in which you testified were plaintiff's cases."

"Is that right?"

"Move to strike," interjected Nagel, "Argumentative, and no question is pending."

"Sustained. The jury will disregard the answer." Nagel was right. There was no question. But the jury also would not disregard the fact that Lester was beginning to look biased.

"Dr. Lester, in formulating your opinion, you testified that you evaluated all peer-reviewed studies on the subject of the effects of solitary confinement, sensory deprivation and overstimulation on suicidal impulses, is that correct?"

"Yes, I did."

"And, based on those studies, you formulated an opinion, within a reasonable degree of medical certainty, is that correct?"

"Yes, that's correct."

"Would you say, doctor, that it is more likely than not that your opinion is correct?"

"Yes, I would."

"So then, it would follow, would it not, that at least 51% of that data supports your opinion?"

"Yes, I would comfortably say that it does."

"Would it also follow, Dr. Lester, that, if 51% of the data supports your opinion, 49% of it does not?"

"Objection, calls for a legal conclusion," said Nagel.

Lester looked like he had just gotten a whiff of some rotten meat. He paused, and then answered. This was not his only case, or his only client.

"It would appear so."

Nagel took Lester through a thorough redirect in order to rehabilitate him, but, if the jury had been paying at least 50% attention to Brent's cross-examination, it had to have made an impression.

"The defense rests, Your Honor."

The next day would be devoted to final argument and instructions to the jury on what law to apply to the facts they were to determine. Brent and Rick high-fived each other outside the courtroom, in the corridor, but both of them knew full well that, even though Brent had ripped Dr. Lester a "new one," the game was far from over.

As they spoke to the press outside the courtroom, they were unaware that a little Marine with a huge chip on his shoulder was following them.

CHAPTER FIFTY-FIVE

There would be no interruptions of Brent's concentration the night before final argument. He had made a long outline of the points he wanted to cover, knowing full well that, once the argument got flowing, he would break from the outline and it would come from the heart. Still, he had to be prepared and that meant going over every small detail and thinking how to emphasize the details to the jury. Brent refused all of Rick's overtures to get together and discuss the case. Sitting in a bar or outdoor café was not his idea of final argument preparation. Brent and Rick drove together back to Santa Barbara, which gave them time to catch up.

"So, bring me up to date on the creepy Marine."

"I talked to him, but he doesn't scare easily. Think I just pushed his buttons."

"Oh, great. Do you think he has anything to do with the case?"

"Don't know, but he sure does have an abnormal interest in it."

"I know. I see him smirking every time Nagel scores a point in trial."

"He did a tour in Iraq. Saw some fucked up shit, apparently. Hates Muslims. He blames them for the deaths of several of his buddies who were blown up by insurgents."

"So, he's got a bone to pick. But why this case?"

"Nearest I can figure, he was part of the Marine guard at Gitmo. No connection to the jail. I guess he just heard stuff on base that got his dander up."

"So, no connection to the case in any real sense?"

"Not that I can see. He's just a nut. I alerted the U.S. Marshal's Security Service and the court staff about his background. They have no right to keep him out of the courtroom, but I thought they should be aware."

The conversation made the long drive home seem shorter. Brent gave Rick his last minute assignments and reminders, but at this point, he knew there wasn't much more that an investigator could do to help the case. It was all up to him now. When they got to Brent's house on Harbor Hills Lane, Rick insisted on coming in.

"Dude, I don't have time to socialize," Brent said, irritatingly.

"Relax, I'm just doing my security thing."

Rick gave the house the once over for security, and then left Brent to his preparation. He got in his car, drove the neighborhood looking for anything suspicious, and, finding nothing out of order, parked his car far enough from Brent's house so he could see it, but could not be seen himself. It was going to be a long night.

Brent fed and petted the cat, took a shower and, being proactive, called Debbie Does Dallas to warn her that this would be one night he would have to spend alone.

"Are you sure?" she pleaded.

"Deb, I have to prepare."

"Come over here and I guarantee you'll walk into court with a smile on your face tomorrow."

"A smile won't win the case."

"Suit yourself. Good luck tomorrow."

"Thanks, Deb."

Brent toiled over his final argument, pausing only for a "box lunch" he had grabbed on the way home for dinner. Outside in his car, Rick worked on his own box lunch dinner while he continued his stake out. He didn't expect anything to happen, but if it did, he would be prepared.

**

At about 3 o'clock in the morning, Rick's tired eyes came back to life as he noticed a beige Toyota Yaris pull up on the cross street, Harbor Hills Drive, and kill the lights. He got out his night vision binoculars to focus in on the occupants of the car. There was only one, but Rick couldn't get a good view of his face.

The driver stayed in the car for a long time, drinking what looked like a beer or soda. Then, he put on a mask and exited the vehicle.

"Oh shit," exclaimed Rick to himself, as he slipped out of his own car and took a place behind the hedge of Brent's next-door neighbor.

The suspect was wearing dark clothing, and was carrying a bag. Rick didn't know if it was a burglar or what, but there was no way he was getting anywhere near Brent's house. As the suspect crept up too close to the house, Rick popped out of the bushes, drew his gun, and shouted, "Freeze!"

The suspect turned and ran back toward his car with Rick in hot pursuit. Rick tackled him right as he reached the Yaris, and slammed him up against the car. The suspect wiggled out of Rick's hold, took a few paces back and pulled a knife.

"Drop the knife, motherfucker. I will shoot you," warned Rick.

"Go ahead," said the little shit, in a gruff, obviously disguised voice.

"Drop the knife! I'm not going to tell you one more time!" Rick didn't want to shoot this little fuck, but he would if he had to. The lights in the neighboring house went on, and Rick knew it would be only a matter of time before the police arrived.

Instead of dropping the knife, the suspect charged at Rick with it, and Rick moved out of the way to avoid being stabbed.

"You think I'm afraid of you, asshole?" asked the suspect, as he waved the knife in front of Rick.

Obviously not, thought Rick. *I just may have to shoot this guy after all.*

"The next time you charge me will be your last," said Rick, matter-of-factly.

The suspect, either sensing that Rick would not shoot, or not caring either way, backed away from Rick slowly at first, then turned and ran. Rick ran after him, down the street, and through a neighboring backyard, which bordered on a vast chaparral.

Rick could see the suspect as he escaped into the hills, where he blended in like a coyote. There was no way he could find him, and it would be suicide to run into the darkness with a maniac lying in wait with a knife, so Rick went back to the car to wait for the police.

***

The Yaris came up as reported stolen. Rick thought to himself, *if you're going to steal a car, why a Yaris?* The car was clean. Nothing was in it that would give away the identity of the suspect. The paperwork with the police took about an hour, and the cops stayed until the tow truck came to tow the car to the impound lot. Rick, exhausted, went back to his stakeout post in case the coyote came back.

CHAPTER FIFTY-SIX

Brent took the podium for his introductory argument. In this argument, he would put his case together for the jury. After Nagel's final argument, Brent would take the podium again in rebuttal. Brent stood, silently for a moment, looking at the jury, then spoke.

"Ladies and Gentlemen, this case is about freedom. The defense will tell you that terrorism has threatened our freedom, and, in order to keep that freedom, we all have to come together and make sacrifices. But, in making the sacrifices that the Government asks us to make, we are not protecting our freedom. We are giving away our freedom in exchange for a false sense of security.

"I'm sure that all of you have heard about your "Constitutional Rights." Actually, you don't have any "Constitutional Rights." In 1791, the first Congress, recognizing that we humans have certain inalienable rights that *nobody* has the right to take away, drafted ten amendments to the United States Constitution that we call the "Bill of Rights." The Bill of Rights wasn't enacted to give us any rights. It was enacted so the Government could not take away from us any rights that we already had."

Brent scanned the faces of the jury to ascertain whether they were paying attention. He sensed that they were, and continued.

"When the United States military arrested Ahmed Khury and threw him into Guantanamo Bay Detention Camp, the Government denied him his right to counsel guaranteed by the Sixth Amendment. They also denied him his right to a speedy trial, to confront the witnesses against him, to a trial by jury, and the right to be informed of what he was charged with. They denied him his right to trial by jury, guaranteed by the Fifth Amendment, his right to due process of the law by holding him indefinitely with no charge, and his coerced confession violated his privilege against self-incrimination.

"Finally, and most importantly, by beating him, treating him as less than human, depriving him of sensory input, overloading his senses, force-feeding and torturing him, the Government denied Ahmed his Eighth Amendment guarantee: To be free from cruel and unusual punishment.

"By breaking into her home without a warrant, eavesdropping on her private telephone conversations, emails, library and bank records, and social networking sites, the Government has also denied Catherine Khury her Fourth Amendment guarantee against unreasonable searches and seizures. The Government denied her this constitutional guarantee by using unconstitutional powers granted it by the USA Patriot Act. Ladies and Gentlemen, the twelve of you have a much more important responsibility than deciding this one case. This case gives not the just opportunity, but *imposes on you the responsibility* of safeguarding these important rights that have been taken away from all of us by the Government, which asserts that it has the authority to suspend the guarantees of the Constitution, so long as it does so outside of the United States. You must do this by declaring that the Patriot Act's amendment to the Foreign Intelligence Surveillance Act violated Catherine's Fourth Amendment guarantees."

By now Brent had broken from his outline, and was delivering his message from the heart. He pounded on the podium to emphasize his next point, with each phrase. "You have the responsibility to deliver a clear message to the Government that we, as human beings, in the United States of America, should be a beacon of freedom to every other country in the world, as we have been for the past 200 years, and that *nobody, no matter what they are accused of doing*, should *ever* be treated the way Ahmed and Catherine were treated. And you deliver this message with a verdict in favor of Catherine Khury and her children and against the Government.

"Not only was Ahmed denied his constitutionally guaranteed rights, he was also denied the rights that any enemy soldier captured fighting against the United States would get pursuant to the Geneva Conventions of 1949. Article 3 of the Geneva Conventions prohibits detention practices that are cruel, degrading, or humiliating."

Brent outlined all the rights of prisoners of war guaranteed by the Geneva Conventions that had been denied to Ahmed. He went over the definitions of torture under the law and contrasted how the Government defined torture in their own illegal way. He summarized how the Government had denied Ahmed his constitutionally guaranteed rights. He went over the medical evidence in detail.

Brent paused, then went on to conclude how he saw the law as applied to each element of evidence in the case, pointing to a chart for each point of the case against the Government for Ahmed's wrongful death, and the Patriot Act's violation of Catherine's constitutionally guaranteed rights.

"Ladies and Gentlemen, the medical evidence points to only one conclusion: That Ahmed Khury was negligently force-fed, which resulted in his aspiration of liquid nutrients. Because the Government failed to follow reasonable medical standards of practice, it resulted in his death, and the Government is responsible for that death. Do we know exactly every step of what happened? No, of course not. We were not there. But all you have to determine as jurors is that it was more likely than not that, because of the lack of physical evidence of death by hanging that the hanging was just a cover up made to look like Ahmed committed suicide.

"Let's be logical about this. Ahmed was waiting for the ruling on his habeas corpus petition. If he had but one glimmer of hope that the key to his prison would be delivered to him, why would he commit suicide?

"And if you decide that a preponderance of the evidence does not point to death during the force-feeding, Ladies and Gentlemen, you don't have to award a verdict to the defense. That is because there is overwhelming evidence that the cruel torture that Ahmed had been subjected to twenty-four hours a day during his indefinite detention, would have driven anyone to despair, and that despair was enough to create an irresistible impulse to commit suicide.

"How do you send this message to the Government with your verdict? There is only one way. You award enough money to Catherine to make it hurt and embarrass the Government for what it has done, in your name, to shame the United States. The terrorist attack on September 11th, 2001 was a terrible tragedy, and the terrorists responsible for it should be punished. But, in this case, the only ones who have been punished are citizens of the United States: Catherine and Ahmed's lives have been destroyed for *nothing*.

"No amount of money will bring Ahmed back to Catherine and her two children. We can't give Catherine back her partner. We can't give Karen a father to walk her down the aisle at her wedding. We can't give Cameron a father to play ball with or teach him how to drive. That is lost forever. . But we can make sure that the financial security that was ripped away from them is restored. We can only give them back this financial security that they have lost from the loss of their provider; to compensate them for the loss of his love and affection, and for the suffering that Ahmed experienced. It's a shame that we cannot give them more than that."

Brent took every second of his allotted argument time, then handed over the podium to Timothy Nagel.

CHAPTER FIFTY-SEVEN

Timothy Nagel took the podium, waving the flag and invoking patriotic religion.

"Ladies and Gentlemen, as you deliberate on the issues presented in this case, I ask you to remember the 3,000 innocent people whose lives were wiped out by a vicious terrorist attack on September 11th, 2001, and how many fathers, mothers, uncles, aunts, brothers and sisters were lost to so many innocent families.

"These terrorist networks are the most formidable enemy the United States has ever had. We are at war, Ladies and Gentlemen, and throughout history, in times of war, the Government has called upon us to gather together as a society and fight the enemy together. Some of your parents and grandparents made sacrifices so we could end the fascist tyranny of Nazi Germany in World War II. Now it is our turn to make sacrifices so we can win the War on Terror.

"The War on Terror is not a conventional war in any sense of the word. The enemy hides in terrorist networks and sleeper cells in many different countries. We cannot go attack an enemy who lies in wait and hides behind no official sovereign flag. That is why the Congress gave the president the authorization to use military force to seek out and destroy these enemy networks in any country that harbors them, and to punish the harboring country accordingly. It is within this framework of these war powers granted the president that a different system had to be set up for catching, holding, trying and punishing terrorists.

"Military tribunals are nothing new, Ladies and Gentlemen. They were formed to try the war criminals of Nazi Germany and they have been formed to try the terrorist criminals of our time. The rights of detainees in Guantanamo Bay like Mr. Khury have to be balanced against the rights of the people of the United States of America to be free from terrorism. It is either us or them, and if we err on any side, I am sure that we all agree that it would be better not to let a guilty terrorist go back to killing innocent people."

Nagel outlined with precision the evidence in the case, with the use of illustrations as Brent had, and, just as everything Brent had said made sense, everything that Nagel said seemed to make sense as well. The jury faced an incredibly difficult job.

Nagel went over all the testimony, pointing the jury to the conclusions he wanted them to make. It was a thorough and convincing presentation.

"Ladies and Gentlemen, you have heard the medical experts testify. The plaintiff has a burden in this case to prove that it was more likely than not that Mr. Khury's death was caused by negligent medical practices. To buy the plaintiff's story, you have to believe that there was an elaborate cover up to make Khury's death look like suicide. However, the plaintiff has not presented one iota of evidence that there was any such cover up. They are asking you to make a giant leap to make that inference which is not supported by *any* evidence. That is impossible to do.

"They next ask you to believe that solitary confinement and its corollary, sensory deprivation, and overstimulation, such as bright lights and music can drive a man to uncontrollable impulses of suicide. Ladies and Gentlemen, you have heard the medical evidence and opinions of experts that this cannot happen unless the person had a mental condition to begin with. And even though Mr. Khury's condition, whatever that was, was not discovered by psychiatrists at Guantanamo, as you have heard from the experts, it is impossible to detect suicide from some patients, and every precaution was taken to check on Mr. Khury every one to three minutes. That is a very high standard of care, Ladies and Gentlemen. Sadly, it took very little time for Mr. Khury to take his own life, something that he must have planned in advance. It doesn't make the Government responsible. The fact that the staff checked on his safety diligently is absolutely contrary to any deliberate indifference to his safety.

"Finally, as we have pointed out, the USA Patriot Act has been upheld in every court in this country where it has been challenged. We have outlined the reasons why the search of Mrs. Khury's home was authorized by law, and, again, we must balance the rights of one individual against the greater good. That is what I would like each and every one of you to do today.

"As you deliberate, deliberate as an American. Deliberate as an individual who is against terrorism and who supports the military and the president in this difficult War on Terror.

And, remember, we did not attack. We were the ones who were attacked. Thank you."

CHAPTER FIFTY-EIGHT

Brent carefully and methodically refuted every argument that Timothy Nagel had made, taking care not to repeat anything the jury had already heard. He closed the rebuttal with an emotional appeal.

"Ladies and Gentlemen, one of the founding fathers of our country, James Madison, said, "The means of defense against foreign danger have been always the instruments of tyranny at home. Among the Romans it was a standing maxim to excite a war, whenever a revolt was apprehended. Throughout all Europe, the armies kept up under the pretext of defending, have enslaved the people."

"When Madison said this, he knew that he, Thomas Jefferson, Benjamin Franklin, and all the other statesmen who formed this country formed the Government to answer to the people, not the other way around. When they set up three branches of government with checks and balances, they did this so that no one branch would get any more powerful than the other.

"What we see in this case is an abuse of power by an over-zealous president, and that abuse of power must be stopped. It is making the United States of America, once a beacon for liberty and freedom and an example for every other democracy to follow, into an aggressive country that does not respect its own laws and does not play by its own principles. When the failure to follow its own rules results in the Government's destruction of lives of its own citizens, as in this case, it is unacceptable, and you need to send a clear message to your Government with this verdict that the United States is a good and humane nation, which does not torture prisoners of war. We are a nation of laws, a nation which respects our fellow humans and the rights of our own citizens, as well as the rights of citizens of other countries.

"When you deliberate, remember that Ahmed Khury could have been one of your neighbors, taken without charge and held indefinitely without due process of law, and tortured until it led logically to his death. That death was the proximate result of the negligence of his captors, by treatment that was fully sanctioned by the Department of Defense and the President of the United States himself.

"Remember that the FBI broke into Catherine's home, without a search warrant, because they suspected criminal activity was afoot. This would not have been evidence enough for any judge to grant them a warrant. Ladies and Gentlemen, the evidence is clear. Catherine Khury has met her burden of proof. You must award damages in the amount of a minimum of $9 million to Catherine Khury for the loss of her husband as a provider, tripled to $27 million on account of the loss of his love, affection, and attention, and his pain and suffering. You must declare that Catherine Khury's constitutionally guaranteed right to be secure in her person, papers and place of abode was violated by the implementation of the USA Patriot Act. It is the only right thing to do."

Judge Henley read the jury a set of written instructions on the law they were to apply to the evidence they heard. They would take the written instructions into the jury room to begin their deliberations. The lawyers would be contacted if the jury had reached a verdict, was unable to make a decision, or had a question. Until then, the only thing that could be done was to wait for them.

CHAPTER FIFTY-NINE

The only thing worse than waiting for a jury, sometimes, is hearing their verdict. During the trial, it is prohibited for the lawyers to talk to the jurors, but afterwards, it is fair game. Brent opted out, more often than not however, because sometimes it was too scary to hear how they came to their verdict. They are supposed to apply the law to the facts, but with a jury that process is filtered through an emotional quagmire of biases and prejudices.

Brent sent Catherine home, and he and Rick hung around the courthouse just in case. They would have to remain close to L.A. for the next few days, as their time to report to court once a verdict or question has been announced was limited.

***

Three days later, the court called Brent about 11:30 and indicated that the jury had reached a verdict. They were to report to court for the announcement after the lunch break at 1:30 p.m. Brent called Catherine, who got in her car right away to try to make it to court on time. Now the waiting was even more stressful than before because Brent knew that there was a verdict, but he did not know what it was.

As the doors to the courtroom opened at 1:30, Brent, Rick, Nagel and Cicatto, and members of the press filed in, as did Balls Anderson, who took his usual seat in the back corner of the gallery. He hadn't been present during final arguments, and Brent could not say that he had missed him at all. That guy gave him the creeps, and the far enough away he was, the better.

At 1:45, Catherine came in, and nervously took a seat at the counsel table with Rick. Shortly thereafter, Judge Henley took the bench, and called the jury in. They filed in and took their seats.

"Ladies and gentlemen of the jury, I understand that you have elected a foreperson?"

"Yes, Your Honor," said juror number 3, Thaddeus Arcaro, an automobile worker, as he stood to address the judge.

"Mr. Foreman, have you reached a verdict?" asked the judge.

"Yes, Your Honor."

"Please hand the verdict to the clerk." Arcaro handed over the verdict and sat down. The clerk handed the verdict to the judge, who read it and gave it back to the clerk.

"The clerk will read the verdict."

"Question one: Do you find that defendants were negligent in the administration of the medical procedure known as enteral feeding to the decedent, Ahmed Khury? Answer: No.'"

Brent instantly felt deflated and discouraged. Catherine started to sob. Since question one was answered in the negative, the clerk read question three.

"Question three: Do you find that the defendants were negligent in the detention of the decedent, Ahmed Khury? Answer: Yes."

Nagel frowned, and Brent raised his eyebrows. There was still hope. Tears streamed down Catherine's face.

"Question four: Do you find that the negligence of the defendants was the proximate cause of the death of Ahmed Khury?' Answer: Yes."

From the gallery, Balls Anderson stood up and shouted, "It's not right! It's not right! He ran through the gallery and jumped over the wooden barrier separating it from the court. Rick bounded over the wooden barrier after him, but it was too late. Before Rick or the Bailiff could catch Anderson, he had thrown himself up onto the counsel table and had Brent in a chokehold.

"Stand back! Or I'll break his goddamn neck," he yelled, dragging Brent in front of him as he stepped backward. The Bailiff stood back. A bevvy of bailiffs appeared in the doorway to the gallery, but dared not approach.

"It's not right! It's un-American! You have to change the verdict!" Balls screamed to the jury.

"Sir, let Mr. Marks go and we will talk about the verdict," said Judge Henley. It was a smart thing to say, as it distracted Balls.

"No, no I won't! He has to *pay!*" Balls tightened his chokehold on Brent, who was gasping for air and turning blue. Catherine recoiled in horror, and sat motionless in fear.

398

The Bailiff, taking advantage of the judge's distraction, lunged at Balls with his stun gun drawn and shocked him. Balls instantly released Brent and was tackled by Rick and the Bailiff. The other bailiffs ran and joined the fray.

"Court will recess until order is restored," said the judge. "The jury is excused. The gallery shall be vacated. The parties and counsel will return in fifteen minutes, please."

The members of the press scrambled for the door to report the drama. When Brent and Catherine exited, they were swamped with questions.

***

When court recommenced, Catherine had already cried herself out. It was if a tremendous weight had been suddenly lifted from her shoulders. Maybe now she would be able to grieve. The jury was called back in and took their seats, and Judge Henley spoke to them.

"Ladies and Gentlemen, I am very saddened by what happened here today. A courtroom is a place where a civilized society settles its disputes without resorting to violence. If this had happened at any time before you had reached a verdict, I would have to declare a mistrial. Thankfully that did not happen and we can continue with the process. I thank each and every one of you for being a part of it."

The court went through the motions of obtaining the verdict again and the clerk continued to read it.

"Question five: What is the amount of damages sustained for loss of financial support from the decedent, Ahmed Khury to the plaintiff, Catherine Khury? Answer: $6,000,000.

"Question six: What is the amount of damages for the loss of benefits that plaintiff, Catherine Khury would have expected to receive from the decedent, Ahmed Khury? Answer: $500,000.

"Question seven: What is the amount of damages for the loss of the decedent, Ahmed Khury's love, companionship, comfort, care, assistance, protection, affection, society, sexual relations and moral support to the plaintiff, Catherine Khury? Answer: $6,000,000.

"Question eight: What is the amount of damages for plaintiff Catherine Khury's grief, sorrow, or mental anguish? Answer: $6,000,000.

"Question nine: What is the amount of damages for the decedent Ahmed Khury's pain and suffering?' Answer: $1,000,000.

"Question ten: Do you find that the electronic surveillance of the plaintiff, Catherine Khury, under section 1804 of the Foreign Intelligence Surveillance Act, as amended by the USA Patriot Act, violated plaintiff Catherine Khury's Fourth Amendment guarantee to be free from unreasonable searches and seizures? Answer: Yes.

"Question eleven: Do you find that the physical search of Catherine Khury's home pursuant to section 1823 of the Foreign Intelligence Surveillance Act, as amended by the USA Patriot Act, violated Catherine Khury's Fourth Amendment guarantee against unreasonable searches and seizures? Answer: Yes."

The jury had spoken. It was a $19,500,000 verdict and the jury had thrown out a chunk of the Patriot Act. After polling the jury, they were excused and the admonition of speaking to them was lifted. Nagel and Cicatto shook Brent's hand. Catherine hugged Brent. In the corridor, she hugged every member of the jury who had stayed behind.

EPILOGUE

The County of Santa Barbara passed a resolution for a monument in honor of Ahmed to be placed in the courtyard of the Santa Barbara courthouse. Catherine paid for the construction of the monument, which was a classic fountain called, "The Ahmed Khury Freedom Fountain." Members of the mosques and Islamic schools in the area were invited to the dedication of the memorial, which was intended to be a symbol of tolerance.

At the dedication, Catherine called upon the new president, Barack Obama, to implement the presidential order he had signed on January 23, 2009, to close Guantanamo Bay Detention Camp within one year. The camp remains open to this day, with many detainees having no hope of ever regaining their freedom.

AFTERWORD

Of course, the story of Ahmed Khury is fictional, but it is based on solid historical research. If you care to read on, I have summarized some of the research. If not, I would like to ask you now to please leave a review. If you scroll to the last page, you will be prompted to do so. Also, there are excerpts of *Predatory Kill,* the first novel in the Brent Marks series and my first novel, *An Involuntary Spy.* Finally, I love to get email from my readers. Please feel free to send me one at info@kennetheade.com. I would also like you to join my mailing list, for advance notice of new books, free excerpts, free books and updates. I will never spam you. Please subscribe here: http://bit.do/mailing-list.

Amnesty International has called the Guantanamo Bay Detention Camp the "gulag of our time." Since President Obama's order to close the camp within one year on January 23, 2009, it has remained open because the president decided to amass political capital to use for his domestic agenda, which included "Obamacare."

On January 7, 2011, Obama signed the 2011 Defense Authorization Bill, which placed restrictions on transferring prisoners to the United States. As of May 2014, there were 149 detainees being held, at a cost to the Government of roughly $1.9 million per detainee. 46 of them have been declared by the Government to be too dangerous to release, but they cannot be tried for any crime because there is insufficient evidence to try them.

Approximately half of the detainees held today have been cleared for release, but may never regain their freedom. Many of their native countries have refused to repatriate them, and, because of the new legislation, they cannot be transferred to prisons in the United States.

After September 11, 2001, torture was official U.S. policy under George Bush, authorized at the highest levels of government. Evidence of its continued and systematic practice continues to surface to this day.

On September 17, 2001, George Bush signed a secret finding empowering the CIA to capture, kill, or interrogate al-Qaeda Leaders." It also authorized establishing a secret global network of facilities to detain and interrogate them without guidelines on proper treatment. Around the same time, Bush approved a secret "high-value target list" of about two dozen names. He also gave CIA free reign to capture, kill and interrogate terrorists not on the list.

On November 13, 2001, the White House issued a Military Order regarding the "Detention, Treatment, and Trial of Certain Non-Citizens in the War on Terror." It determined that "an extraordinary emergency exists for national defense purposes that this emergency constitutes an urgent and compelling Government interest and that issuance of this order is necessary to meet the emergency." It defined targeted individuals as al Qaeda and others for aiding or abetting acts of international terrorism or harboring them. These individuals were to be denied access to U.S. or other courts and instead tried by military commission with the power to convict by the concurrence of two-thirds of its members.

On December 28, 2001, Deputy Assistant Attorney Generals Patrick Philbin and John Yoo, sent a Memorandum to General Counsel, Department of Defense, and William Haynes II entitled: "Possible Habeas Jurisdiction over Aliens Held in Guantanamo Bay, Cuba." It said that federal courts have no jurisdiction over and cannot review Guantanamo detainee mistreatment or mistaken arrest cases. It further stated that international laws don't apply in the "War on Terror." This laid the groundwork for abuses in all U.S. military prisons.

On January 18, 2002, Bush issued a "finding" stating that prisoners suspected of being al Qaeda or Taliban members are "enemy combatants" and unprotected by the Third Geneva Convention. They were to be denied all rights and treated "to the extent…consistent with military necessity." Torture was thus authorized. The 2006 Military Commissions Act – also known as the "torture authorization act" – later created the Geneva-superseded category of "unlawful enemy combatant" to deny them any chance for judicial fairness.

International law expert Francis Boyle stated that "this quasi-category created a universe of legal nihilism where human beings (including US citizens) can disappear, be detained incommunicado, denied access to attorneys and regular courts, tried by kangaroo courts, executed, tortured, assassinated and subjected to numerous other manifestations of State Terrorism" on the pretext of as protecting national security.

On January 19, 2002 Donald Rumsfeld sent a memo to the Joint Chiefs of Staff entitled: "Status of Taliban and al Qaeda." It stated that these detainees "are not entitled to prisoner of war status for purposes of the Geneva Conventions of 1949." It gave commanders enormous latitude to treat prisoners "to the extent appropriate with military necessity" as they saw fit.

On January 25, 2002, Alberto Gonzales issued a memo to George W. Bush, which called the Geneva Conventions "quaint" and "obsolete" and said the administration could ignore them in interrogating prisoners. He also outlined plans to try prisoners in military commissions and to deny them all protections under international law, including due process, habeas corpus rights, and the right to appeal. In December 2002, Donald Rumsfeld concurred by approving a menu of interrogation practices allowing anything short of what would cause organ failure.

On February 7, 2002, the White House issued an Order "outlining treatment of al-Qaeda and Taliban detainees." It stated that, "none of the provisions of the Geneva Conventions apply to our conflict with al-Qaida or the Taliban in Afghanistan "or elsewhere throughout the world."

A plethora of similar memos followed covering much the same ground, allowing all measures that had been banned under international and U.S. law, including the 1994 Torture Statute and the Torture Act of 2000, and the 1996 War Crimes Act, which imposes a penalty of up to life in prison or death for persons convicted of committing war crimes within or outside the US. Torture is a high war crime, the highest after genocide.

Two other memos were written by John Yoo, Alberto Gonzales, Jay Bybee (now a federal court of appeals justice in the Ninth Circuit) and David Addington, Dick Cheney's former legal counsel. One was for the CIA on August 2, 2002. It argued that interrogators should be free to use harsh measures amounting to torture. It said federal laws prohibiting these practices don't apply when dealing with al-Qaeda because of the presidential authorization to use force during wartime. It also denied that U.S. or international law applies in overseas interrogations. It essentially "legalized" anything in the "War on Terror" and authorized lawlessness and supreme presidential power.

On March 14, 2003, the group issued another memo entitled, "Military Interrogation of Alien Unlawful Combatants Held Outside the United States." This became known as "the

Torture Memo" because it swept away all legal restraints and authorized military interrogators to use extreme measures amounting to torture. It also gave the president as Commander-in-Chief "the fullest range of power...to protect the nation." It stated he "enjoys complete discretion in the exercise of his authority in conducting operations against hostile forces."

Military law expert and Yale University lecturer, Eugene Fidell called the memo "a monument to executive supremacy and the imperial presidency, and a road map for the Pentagon to avoid any prosecutions." It denied that due process was applicable as well as virtually all other constitutional protections. It argued against any prohibition banning "cruel and unusual treatment."

In 2004, the head of the Office of Legal Counsel, Jack Goldsmith, rescinded the Memorandum, saying it showed an "unusual lack of care and sobriety in legal analysis and seemed more an exercise of sheer power than reasoned analysis."

Nevertheless, other administration documents authorized continued use of practices generally reflecting Yoo's and Bybee's views. They authorized the infliction of "intense pain or suffering" short of what would cause "serious physical injury so severe that death, organ failure, (loss of significant body functions), or permanent damage" may result.

The president's July 20, 2006 Executive Order was one such document, entitled "Interpretation of the Geneva Conventions Common Article 3 as Applied to a Program of Detention and Interrogation Operated by the Central Intelligence Agency." It pertained to "a member or part of or supporting al Qaeda, the Taliban, or associated organizations who may have information that could assist in detecting, mitigating, or preventing terrorist attacks...within the United States or against its Armed Forces or other personnel, citizens, or facilities, or against allies or other countries cooperating in the war on terror..."

It authorized the Director of CIA to determine appropriate interrogation practices. Based on what is now known, they included sleep deprivation, waterboarding or simulated drowning, stress positions (including painfully extreme ones), prolonged isolation, sensory deprivation and/or overload, beatings, electric shocks, induced hypothermia, and other measures that can cause irreversible physical and psychological harm, including psychoses.

In a secret 2007 report, the International Committee of the Red Cross concluded that CIA interrogators had tortured high-level al Qaeda prisoners. Abu Zubaydah was one, a reputed close associate of Osama bin Laden and a Guantanamo detainee. He was confined in a box "so small (that) he had to double up his limbs in the fetal position" and stay that way. He and others were also "slammed against the walls," waterboarded to simulate drowning, and given other harsh and abusive treatment.

The report also said Khalid Shaikh Mohammed, the alleged chief 9/11 planner, was kept naked for over a month, "…alternately in suffocating heat and in a painfully cold room." Most excruciating was a practice of shackling prisoners to the ceiling and forcing them to stand for as long as eight hours. Other techniques included prolonged sleep deprivation, "bright lights and eardrum-shattering sounds 24 hours a day."

Bernard Barrett of the International Red Cross declined to comment but confirmed that Red Cross personnel regularly visit Guantanamo detainees, including high-level ones. They also "have an ongoing confidential dialogue with members of the US intelligence community, and we would share any observations or recommendations with them."

A Presidential July 20, 2007 Executive Order 13440 interpreted the Geneva Conventions Common Article 3 as Applied to a Program of

413

Detention and Interrogation Operated by the Central Intelligence Agency. The Executive Order is noteworthy for what it doesn't say, not for what it says. Its language is reassuring but avoids stopping short of the administration's official policy of torture:

"Noncombatants, including "members of armed forces who laid down their arms....shall in all circumstances be treated humanely..."

"...The following acts are prohibited at any time and in any place...

- Violence to life and person (including) murder, mutilation, cruel treatment and torture
- Taking of hostages
- Humiliating and degrading treatment
- Sentencing or executing detainees "without previous judgment pronounced by a regularly constituted court affording all the judicial guarantees...recognized as indispensable by civilized peoples" and
- Assuring wounded and sick are cared for.

Various human rights organizations have reacted to this Executive Order. The Washington Director of Human Rights

First, Elisa Massimino, the head of *Human Rights First,* said the Order "fails to make clear whether (CIA authorized) interrogation techniques are still permitted." If the CIA interprets the Order "as authorization to continue using techniques such as waterboarding, stress positions, hypothermia, sensory deprivation and overload, sleep deprivation and isolation, it sends a powerful – and dangerous – message" that these and other banned practices are permissible. Bush's Executive Order avoided clarity and left considerable leeway for abuse.

The executive continued to deny all basic rights to detainees, including the constitutional guarantee of habeas corpus, and the Congress went along with it, in passing a series of Acts of Congress attempting to limit this constitutional guarantee.

In 2004, the United States Supreme Court held, in *Rasul v. Bush,* that the habeas corpus jurisdiction of United States federal courts extended to Guantanamo Bay.

In 2004, the Court also held, in *Hamdi v. Rumsfeld,* that due process mandated that an alleged enemy combatant held on U.S. soil be entitled to a due process challenge of his enemy combatant status.

In June 2006 the Supreme Court, in *Hamdan v. Rumsfeld* threw out section 1005a of the Detainee Treatment Act denying the right of an alien detainee to habeas corpus, and ruled that the structure and procedures of the military commissions established to try detainees violated both the Uniform Code of Military Justice and Common Article 3 of the Geneva Conventions had been violated. Congress passed and Bush signed into law the Military Commissions Act in October 2006, overriding the Supreme Court's decision.

In 2008, the Supreme Court threw out the Act's prohibition of the federal courts' jurisdiction to hear detainees' habeas corpus petitions as an unconstitutional suspension of habeas corpus in *Boumedine v. Bush.*

District Court Judge Aiken threw out two sections of the Patriot Act that modified the Foreign Intelligence Surveillance Act in *Mayfield v. United States,* but her decision was rendered moot on appeal when the Ninth Circuit Court of Appeal decided that Mayfield could not pursue his declaratory relief claim after he had settled with the Government.

The "War on Terror" is still on, and is still being used as an excuse to extend the broad brush of governmental power. The USA Patriot Act was designed to be temporary, but has been reauthorized in 2005 and 2006. On February 27, 2010, President Obama signed into law legislation reauthorizing three controversial sections of the Act relating to roving wiretaps, lone wolf surveillance and seizure of property and records. On May 26, 2011, he signed into law the Patriot Sunsets Extension Act to extend key provisions of the Act.

One more thing...

I hope you have enjoyed this book and I am thankful that you have spent the time to get to this point, which means that you must have received something from reading it. If you believe your friends would enjoy this book, I would be honored if you would post your thoughts, and also leave a review on Amazon.

Best Regards,

Kenneth Eade

info@kennetheade.com

BONUS OFFER

Sign up for paperback discounts, advance sale notifications of this and other books and free stuff by going to my website at: www.kennetheade.com. I will never spam you.

ABOUT THE AUTHOR

Author Kenneth Eade, best known for his legal and political thrillers, practiced law for 30 years before publishing his first novel, "An Involuntary Spy." Eade, an up-and-coming author in the legal thriller and courtroom drama genre, has been described by critics as "one of our strongest thriller writers on the scene, and the fact that he draws his stories from the contemporary philosophical landscape is very much to his credit." Critics have also said that "his novels will remind readers of John Grisham, proving that Kenneth Eade deserves to be on the same lists with the world's greatest thriller authors."

Says Eade of the comparisons: "John Grisham is famous for saying that sometimes he likes to wrap a good story around an important issue. In all of my novels, the story and the important issues are always present."

Eade is known to keep in touch with his readers, offering free gifts and discounts to all those who sign up at his web site, www.kennetheade.com.

.

CPSIA information can be obtained
at www.ICGtesting.com
Printed in the USA
LVOW04s1617110816
499999LV00021B/506/P